No Strings For The Summer

Dae Storm

Authors Note

I hope you all enjoy reading this story as much as I did writing it. There is very few troubling topics covered in this novella, but here are a list of them so that anyone who needs to prepare themselves before reading, can.

Work place discrimination based on sexuality, age, and disability is referenced.

Minor harassment by an unknown character.

1

Olivia

"Oh, God," I groaned into the cab window. My face was squished up against the glass. The sunlight poured onto my face, and it only made the throbbing in my head worse.

Besides the driver, I was alone in the car and grateful for that. I wasn't sure I could handle much small talk.

"It's too bright," I mumbled, picking my head up and trying to turn it away from the window. Instead, I knocked it against the glass. I cringed and squeezed my eyes shut tighter.

"Too many shots on the plane?" the driver, Cal, asked.

I swallowed hard and finally gathered the strength to remove my face from the window and lean my head back against the seat instead. The window was cooler, but the seat was softer, and there was less sun to violate my eyes.

"Mhm," I replied. The wind that billowed through the front windows and back to me was both refreshing and nauseating.

Cal just laughed, and I heard him tap on the steering wheel. "Should've saved the fun for tonight!"

I sighed. "Yeah. Even if it was just the plane, I was excited to finally be on vacation. There were only ten people on the plane, and they kept giving me more."

"Guess they wanted ta spice things up, ay?" Cal suggested.

I just raised my shoulders in a weak shrug.

After a moment, the movement of the car wasn't making me feel as sick, so I dared to crack my eyes open. Nope. I closed them again the second they were open.

I had wanted to enjoy the view of St. Lucia on the way to the hotel, but that idea had flown out of the window.

"Are ya here alone?" Cal asked.

I was too distracted to answer dishonestly, even though I had no idea what his intentions were.

"Yup," I replied with another sigh. "All alone in the peace and quiet."

It was a long moment before he spoke again.

"Well, a pretty thing like you, you better be careful walkin' around alone. If you get into any trouble, call me will ya? My number's in the app."

I squinted at him thorough my partially-open eyes and saw him smiling softly as he looked out of the windshield. He looked old enough to be one of my parents, but I sensed a slightly flirty edge in his tone that told me I could call him even if I wasn't in trouble. I couldn't say his age was really a problem, but his gender was.

Still, I just smiled slightly, making sure he saw it in the rear-view mirror, and closed my eyes again.

Sure, it wasn't the best idea to go on my vacation alone, but the only person I'd want to come with me, my best friend

4

Chelsea, had totally different ideas of a wonderful vacation than me. While I wanted to lie in the tropical sun, she wanted to spend a few weeks in a cabin, snuggled up under a blanket near a fireplace. So, I'd come alone, but I wasn't too concerned as I'd chosen the highest rated hotel.

My hangover had my blonde tresses hanging down over my shoulders, as my scalp was sensitive, but the heat of the island had my thoughts lingering on the hair tie around my wrist. Trading one uncomfortable situation for another, I pulled my hair up into a messy bun just as the cab stopped near the entrance of the hotel.

"You need any help?" Cal asked. I could tell he was really interested in helping me take my things to my room.

"No, thank you," I mumbled, looking at my phone long enough to send him a tip.

I opened the car door just as the trunk popped open and pulled my purse over my shoulder before walking around to it. I grabbed my singular rolling suitcase and small duffel bag and used my elbow to shut the trunk.

Fuck, I wish I hadn't misplaced my sunglasses. I'd be able to buy some once I got inside, but right then the sun was drilling a hole into my head.

By the time I walked the few yards into the slightly cooler hotel lobby, I was in a much worse mood than I'd been in the cab.

Seven other people stood at the desk in the lobby, and I sighed before walking up behind them. Most of them were just chatting at each other. I wasn't even sure they were in line, but one woman, with the most luxurious chestnut curls falling down her back, was talking to the clerk.

I was lost in her hair until I heard what she was saying.

"I absolutely need another room. You must have at least one room with one bed free, right?" It was more a statement than a question, but there was a slight inflection in her tone.

"Ma'am, I'm afraid we don't have any rooms available for you right now. I can let you know if one becomes available."

I rolled my eyes. Of course, I was being kept from my own room because this woman wasn't happy with hers. I tried to maintain some sort of calm while I stood there.

However, the drone of listening to the group talk beside me and the frustrated tone of the woman in front of me was making it hard to just stand there.

"What's wrong with your room?" I asked suddenly. My voice was both harsher than intended and nowhere near as harsh as it could have been.

The woman turned around to look at me, her brow furrowed in confusion. "What?" she asked.

Ignoring the pounding in my head, I forced a smile onto my face. "What's wrong with your room that you need a new one?"

She blinked. "I don't see how that's your business." Her voice was low and her tone raspy yet smooth.

As my face flushed with heat, I realized I had pushed my way into something I normally wouldn't have. I cleared my throat and tried to collect my thoughts. "Well...I guess it isn't, but she's doing all she can to help you. The least you could do is thank her."

The woman eyed me from head to toe, her gray eyes dark and stormy.

She took a slow breath through her nose and folded her arms under her breasts. It took all my strength not to lower my gaze.

"I suppose you're right," she said slowly, her cheeks reddening. "Still, I'd appreciate you staying out of my business." Her nose crinkled, and she turned around to the counter again.

My shoulders were nearly up to my ears with tension. I felt a little like I'd been scolded, but I felt a little better as I overheard her apologize and thank the woman at the desk for trying.

My eyes followed the brunette woman as she walked away from the counter, and I noted the swing of her plush hips as she disappeared from view.

"Do you need help?"

"Mrs...Uh," the clerk said.

I turned to look at the counter. The group that had been to the side of me was slowly moving away while conversing, and I could hear they were talking about what they'd just witnessed. I'd been too caught up to even notice them watching.

"It's Miss, and yes. I'm Olivia Waitts." I sighed. Finally, it was my turn.

After getting checked in, I tossed my bags on the floor at the end of the bed, made sure the room key card was placed where I'd remember it, and face planted onto the bed, kicking my flip-flops off.

"Sweet...baby..." The last word referencing Christ was muffled by the bed.

The cool air conditioning, the darkness, the soft bed—I needed it more than anything else. Still, I forced myself to get up and grab some painkillers, which I downed with about half a bottle of water before curling back up in bed.

Normally, I would have looked around the room, seen what was in the drawers and checked out the TV for a bit before heading out to the beach or maybe a restaurant. But I needed a major lie down before I was going to do any of those things.

There were two things that helped my headaches and hangovers, and I'd already taken the meds...

Snuggled under the blanket, I shimmied out of my denim shorts and let them get lost in the duvet. I stuck my ring and middle fingers into my mouth, wetting them, then slid my perfectly manicured hand into my panties and wasted no time finding my clit. I wasn't in the mood for romancing myself; I needed to get off hard and fast so I could doze off and wake up renewed. Hopefully.

My thighs spread under the covers as I explored my blooming arousal. It wasn't difficult. My mind flicked back to the long gorgeous hair, piercing eyes, and round hips of the woman in the lobby. Instantly my thighs were warm, my face following suit. A bit of guilt about thinking about a woman I didn't even know crossed over me but was quickly replaced by more images. I hadn't been paying attention to it, but now I remembered the scent of her hair wafting toward me as she turned around. Like honey from roses.

I rubbed circles around my clit, feeling the tingling pleasure in my hips and up my spine. Soft moans escaped my lips, and I tilted my head back against the pillow. I didn't even know her name, nor did she know mine, but that wouldn't stop me from imagining her moaning out my own.

My fingers collected my slick juices from my pussy and slid them up around my throbbing bud, making each pass of my fingers even better. I pushed my heels into the mattress and rocked my hips needily against my own hand, barely able to handle the pressure that I already felt building in my cunt. I needed to come so badly that I would have done anything just to get off. I didn't care who heard me, who knew what I was doing.

I chased the pleasure as I stroked and circled my clit eagerly, my hips rolling in time with my movements.

"Oh, fuck me!" I panted for breath. My free hand slid down and gripped at the inside of my plush thigh, my nails digging into the flesh. A shiver ran up my spine, and I wiggled against it.

The ache in my head didn't matter. The disappointment that had been the cab ride was washed from my head, and all I wanted was to feel that wave of relief wash over me.

My moans grew more and more desperate as I got closer to the edge of that orgasm. I could feel it—so close, so...fucking...close.

As my toes curled against the sheet, my hips rocked more furiously, causing the bed to creak in an erratic rhythm underneath me.

"Yes, yes!" I removed my hand from my thigh and grabbed onto one of the wooden bars of the headboard. Soft, low, animistic pants and grunts interrupted my moaning as I ached for my hand to move even faster than it was.

My entire body was so hot that the AC may as well have not even been on.

I felt my pussy clench as that bubble of pressure popped within me, and pleasure rushed around my clit and up my stomach, tingling through my spine. My toes curled even harder, and my entire body tensed for a moment, no sound coming from my mouth.

Finally, I exhaled a heavy breath, followed by panting moans.

The tension eased from my muscles until I was a puddle in the bed. My hand, panties, and a patch of the sheet underneath me were soaking wet.

"Ah, fuck." I took a deep breath and let it out. Again and again.

"Mm."

I laid there in bliss and stared at the ceiling with my eyes half open.

My head already felt better, but I had little time to think about that before I was dozing off. I just barely got my hand out of my panties before everything went dark.

⁂

When my eyes fluttered open, the first thing I noticed was that it didn't feel like an icepick was ramming between them.

The room was still pleasantly dimmed by the thick curtains on the windows, but I could see clearer now. Colors were brighter, less painful, and the sound of the mini-fridge compressor kicking in didn't infuriate me as it might have before.

I licked my lips and realized how thirsty I was. As I forced myself to sit up in bed, the blanket fell from my chest, and the cool air in the room gave me goosebumps. I reached for the water bottle I'd put on the nightstand and downed the other half quickly.

"Well..." I mumbled to myself but didn't continue my thought out loud.

I felt a lot better. Maybe not entirely, but it wasn't anything more water and some food couldn't fix.

Speaking of the devil, my stomach rumbled loudly as I got out of bed. "I know, I know." It continued to grumble as I slipped out of my panties and went digging in my bag for a fresh pair.

I glanced at the clock. It had been three hours. Damn. The sun would be setting in about an hour and a half. It was definitely dinner time.

After a trip to the bathroom, another half bottle of water, and a change into new panties and comfortable shorts, I grabbed the pamphlet I'd been given along with my room key to see where the nearest beach bar and grille was.

Oh, perfect! Seven minute walk from the hotel. Not too bad at all.

I was glad I'd packed my comfortable sandals; I was going to be doing a lot of walking.

I slung my purse over my shoulder, ignoring my slightly sore muscles, and headed to the lobby to buy a new pair of sunglasses first.

The sun wasn't nearly as glaring at this time of day. The sunglasses helped in case my eyes were still sensitive.

I didn't feel my best yet, but I wasn't going to miss out on the beautiful sunset my first night in St. Lucia. In the fucking Caribbean, of all places.

No way.

2

Kathleen

The tropical sun that soaked into my already tan skin did little to ease the aggravation I was feeling. The fact that I had been standing to the side of the gift shop outside of the hotel for thirty minutes, waiting on my coworkers to just pick something, didn't help either.

"You're not going to get anything, Kathy?" Robert said as he spun around in his wheelchair, a t-shirt and keychain in his lap.

I tightened my arms that were folded against my chest. "No."

Christa looked at me, too. Her youthful face was smooth, doe-eyed, and contorted with concern.

"Are you still upset about the room?" she asked. She was holding a seashell necklace with a shark's tooth attached to it, the kind of thing you could get at every gift shop in Florida or California for fuck's sake.

My tongue darted along my lips. "Yes, Christa," I replied, being careful with my words, "I am. They sent four of us here on vacation, the cast-offs—"

Liam turned around as well and cut me off mid-sentence. "I wouldn't say we're cast-offs. Would they send us on an island vacation if we were?"

I took a slow breath through my nose. "Yes. How don't you all see it? We're here for two weeks, the four of us, in one hotel room with two beds." I held up both of my hands, one with two fingers up and one with four fingers up to illustrate my point.

"You and Robert refuse to share a bed," I motioned toward Liam, then Christa, "Christa, you don't want to share a bed with anyone. I'm willing to do anything, even share a bed with one of you," I teased.

Liam's mock pout sat charmingly on his own boyish face.

"Look," I said, "at the office, they assign me the most craptastic cases. You too, Robert. Liam and Christa are only here because they didn't know where the fuck else to put the temps on the company dime while they want on their Big Boys' vacation." I put my hands down at my sides.

The people in front of me looked uncomfortable. Shifting awkwardly on their feet—and chair, and clutching their items.

"I'm over forty and a lesbian, so I'm all but dead to them." I waved toward Robert. "And you're over forty and disabled." Then to Liam I said, "You're...well, honestly, they probably just didn't want you with them because you like us. And you're nineteen and unwilling to sleep with any of them like they hired you for," I finished, motioning toward Christa.

Christa shrugged and nodded gently, her eyes sad.

"Look," I sighed, "I'm fine being here with you three, but I'm not fine with those jackasses sending us here for two weeks, with two beds, and no company food budget while they travel Europe for a month and charge all their meals to the company credit card."

Their faces dropped even more.

"Yeah, that sucks." Christa frowned.

"We'll just have to figure out how to manage for now I guess," Robert said and then turned his wheelchair slightly left and slightly right. "Something I'm good at."

I nodded. There was a long silence; even Liam had nothing to say.

"I'm sorry for being a bitch," I said finally. "You finish picking out your stuff; I'm just going to roam around."

Liam was the last to turn back around toward the gift shop. "We're going to that beach side restaurant later on," he reminded me.

"Uh-huh," I replied and tried to shoot him a smile, but it just ended up half-assed.

I pulled my phone out of my shorts pocket and turned up the brightness all the way so I could see more clearly. Standing a few feet away and walking back and forth along the wooden planks that were sunken into the sand, I scrolled through various social media apps.

Out of curiosity, I decided to peek at my boss's Instagram. Great, he was having a wonderful time.

Scroll. Scroll. More coffee, more dinner, more fancy hotel rooms.

I scrolled until I was past the last four days of his vacation photos and eyed the photos of his home, his dogs, his wife, his children. All so perfect, in an alien sort of way.

I clicked on a photo from last summer that had more likes than usual.

Caption: In St. Lucia at the beach house for the week.
I blinked.

"Wait," I mumbled, eyeing the background. "Motherfucker!" I growled.

Several people around me jumped, but I didn't check to see if my coworkers had heard.

"Fuck! He has a beach house here, and he sent us to a one room hotel!?"

That was it! I couldn't stand near the gift shop anymore. I needed to walk away before I kicked it down, and I was suddenly desperate for a drink.

The scent of the salty ocean and grilled chicken and fish wafted toward me before I had even stepped foot onto the beachfront. I wanted a strong, fruity, cold drink. I really shouldn't, but I was aching for something to soothe my aggravation.

I sighed just thinking about it, keeping my eyes on the bar hut with its colorful roof and trim as my sandals crunched gently on the sand. The hut was only occupied by a few people sitting on stools and chatting. A familiar voice spoke first as I was about to open my mouth.

"Virgin Bloody Mary, please."

I saw the slender face of the young woman who had set me straight several hours before. I hadn't noticed while fuming in the lobby just how vibrant her blonde hair was. It hung in loose, frizzy waves behind her with the sides clipped back. The streaks of lighter blonde practically glowed in the sun.

I realized I was staring, but I couldn't look away until the bartender vied for my attention. Suddenly, I wasn't as interested in the alcohol anymore.

"Oh, ah, virgin Piña colada, thanks," I ordered. A small voice in my head cheered me on.

"You too?" the woman asked and turned to look at me. Her sweet voice was full of amusement at both of us ordering alcoholic drinks sans alcohol.

However, before I could open my mouth, she was wide eyed. "Oh!" She cleared her throat "...You."

The way her face flushed deep red made my entire body even warmer than it already was, and I was looking forward to the cold drink.

"Did you think I might have left?" I teased her.

She blinked her big brown eyes. "N-no, I just didn't expect to see you here. I thought you couldn't get a room." Her voice held a slight edge. She was still annoyed with the situation earlier, clearly.

"Well, you didn't know the whole situation," I replied. I tried not to sound defensive, but it was difficult.

Her shoulders straightened, and she shifted her body away from me, tensing.

I eyed her briefly while she was sliding her drink closer to her.

"Huh, I didn't realize I'd made such a negative impression." I chuckled softly, looking away from her to watch the bartender preparing my drink. I wanted to be certain he didn't forget and put alcohol in it. My lapse in judgment moments before was gone. It often left as quickly as it came.

"No?" she asked, and our eyes met again.

My lips turned down at the edges. "No," I told her, then tilted my head side-to-side. "Well, I suppose I've been fiery lately. It's nothing to do with you or that clerk in the lobby."

Her face flushed deeper as her gaze landed on my ample breasts that were contained only by the snug floral bikini top I was wearing.

"Oh," she mumbled, then sipped at her drink.

I smirked at her. She seemed so embarrassed, though I wasn't sure why.

I looked over and nodded in thanks to the bartender as he set my drink down, and I slid it closer to me as well. I took several quick sips and hummed in satisfaction. Yup, definitely no alcohol. It would've tasted disgusting to me ten years before, but now, it was normal.

"I'm sorry if I was making a scene in there," I finally said.

The young woman's gaze met mine again, and I found myself desperate to stare into her eyes for as long as possible, which surprised me enough that my own face flushed deeper.

She waved her hand. "No, no... It wasn't really my business anyway," she insisted. "I was hung over and just wanted to get to my room."

I nodded twice. "Ah, and I was in the way of that." I pursed my lips. "I guess we both were making a scene."

She chuckled. "I wouldn't say I made a scene."

I held my drink in one hand and leaned against the counter with my other. "You're blushing an awful lot, though. Are you embarrassed?" I asked.

She shook her head quickly but said nothing else while she sipped.

I figured she wasn't interested in talking anymore, so I turned back toward the bar.

"What's your name?" she asked.

Blinking at her in surprise, I told her, "Oh, Kathleen," I told her. "And yours?"

She smiled now, a bright, sweet smile that made me dizzy.

"Guess," she insisted.

I raised a brow. "Guess?"

She rested her elbow on the bar and then her chin in her palm.

"Guess," she repeated herself.

Giving a short laugh, I said, "Alright," then hummed to myself.

My eyes took in her gorgeous hair and soft, heart-shaped face again as I thought. It would be far too cliche of a line to say "Angel," but in that moment that's all I could think of.

"Ariel," I told her. "It's a version of the Hebrew name Ari'el. It means Lion of God."

Her brows lifted. "You think that fits me?" she asked.

I shifted closer to her. "Absolutely, your hair is like...a vibrant lion angel's mane." I felt drunk on her presence and let the words just roll off my tongue.

"My name isn't Ariel, unfortunately," she replied. "It's Olivia. Most of my friends call me Liv."

"Do you like being called Liv?" I asked.

She shrugged. "It's okay."

"I guess I'll need to come up with another name for you then," I replied. My voice was low, huskier.

What was I doing? Olivia was, given her looks, definitely in her mid-twenties and given my luck, most likely straight. Still, as the scent of her skin and hair engulfed me along with the salty breeze, I couldn't pull myself away from her.

"I'm truly sorry about earlier, Olivia," I said.

She smiled softly. Her lips were full and supple. "It's okay."

I looked down at the bar for a second, and remembered what she'd said earlier. "Hung over, huh?" I asked. "You've been here a while?"

Olivia chuckled. "No. I just had too much to drink on the plane; I was really excited about starting my vacation, and I guess they had a lot of drinks prepared but barely any passengers." She stopped with her mouth open slightly. "Sorry, I'm rambling."

I shook my head. "No, no. Don't apologize. Never apologize for talking." My voice was slightly harsher than intended, and I added on a soft smile to blunt my words.

"Thanks." Olivia took a sip of her almost-gone drink.

"I was on that flight, too," I told her.

Olivia started coughing and put her hand on her chest. Before I could even reach out and touch her shoulder, she was waving her hand and clearing her throat. "I just can't believe I didn't see you, and then...the lobby." She sighed and shook her head.

I smirked and tried to move on from the subject to avoid her embarrassment.

"So, that's why you're having a virgin drink? The hangover?" She nodded. "You?"

My heart anxiously skipped a beat. Telling a hot woman on vacation that I'm a recovering alcoholic couldn't possibly be the way to go; but I refused to lie. I refused to be ashamed.

"Ah, no," I said. "I'm ten years sober."

Olivia snorted cold red slushy liquid out of her nose onto her top lip and quickly reached for a napkin. "Oh, my god, I'm okay! I'm just getting into things that aren't my business. Again!"

I would have checked on her, but I was too busy laughing my ass off. I tried to catch my breath as I leaned against the bar with both arms, my head down.

"What?!"

I took a deep breath and tilted my head up. "Nothing, nothing. You're just..." I exhaled. "Fuck, you're really adorable, Olivia." I swallowed hard as I realized what I said.

Something crossed over her beautiful face—recognition? Understanding? I wasn't sure exactly.

"I don't know if I'm getting the right vibes, Kathleen. I've never really...flirted with anyone I didn't already know was queer. But I'm twenty-seven, so I'd like to think I'm firmly out of adorable territory." Olivia started fiddling with the straw of her drink.

Twenty-seven. Huh. Definitely still adorable.

"I'm a lesbian, Olivia, if that's what you're trying to ask," I told her, my pulse racing.

"Oh, thank God."

I smiled and brushed several locks of my curls back into play as well as I could. They'd fallen over my forehead when I was laughing so hard.

"You were flirting with me?" I asked her.

"Kind of. Well...I wanted to," Olivia admitted. "I'm so embarrassed because of what happened earlier." She took a deep breath. "I'm usually a lot more confident; trust me."

"Okay," I replied, "I'll trust you. If you don't apologize or mention what happened in the lobby again for the rest of the night."

By the way Olivia squirmed on her stool, I could guess she was as interested in my company for the rest of the night as I was interested in hers.

21

"Agreed," she said as she held her hand out.

We shook hands. Hers was smaller but rougher than my own. A tingle shot up my palm and into my arm, warm and wanting. I nearly shivered.

"Good," I said, keeping my voice as level as possible.

I watched as she all but sucked every drop of her drink out and then licked the straw. My bikini bottoms were already hot and wet just watching her tongue lap up the remaining juices.

Fuck, this twenty-seven-year-old woman was turning me on like no one else had in years. *Could she really be interested in me?*

I shook the thought off. "Let me buy you another drink. Virgin, of course."

"Oh no, you don't have to!"

"I insist, especially if we're going to be sitting here a while." I smiled.

I slid her drink back up the bar and asked the bartender for another.

"Come on!" I chuckled. "I promise I won't laugh." It was a hard promise to make, though. She was beautiful, funny, sweet. And sexy.

"Okay!" She took a deep breath. "I'll tell you."

My bottom lip caught in my teeth as I stared at her, waiting. This was the most captured I had ever been by a woman I had just met while sober.

"When I imagine what my first night here would be like..." Olivia started, her gaze shifting to the sunset behind us. "...It's a perfect sunset with a warm breeze. A beautiful stranger is whisking me away for—" I watched her face grow darker.

"What?" I asked.

Olivia's chest rose and fell quicker as she finished her sentence. "—Sex on the beach. And I don't mean the drink."

I squeezed my thighs together and reminded myself that I didn't have time to hook up with Olivia; I had dinner with my co-workers to go to.

My pussy didn't seem to care.

"Doesn't everyone dream of being whisked away on an island vacation?" she asked with a laugh.

Oh, fuck it.

I stood up from my seat and slapped the money down to pay for both our drinks.

"What are you doing?" Olivia asked.

I stepped away from her but reached my hand out, motioning with my fingers. "Whisking you away."

She looked at my hand and seemed to debate for a moment before she pulled her purse over her shoulder and took my hand. Olivia's hand in mine was warm and soft. Our fingers intertwined, and we walked side by side on the beach. I was several inches taller than her, my steps larger, so I slowed my pace.

I opened my mouth to speak, but when I looked over and saw the sunset reflecting on her hair and in her eyes, I couldn't remember what I had planned on saying.

We walked like this for a while until the only people nearby were small in my vision.

"That was so stunning," Olivia said. She turned to look at me, smiling, her eyes shining.

"Yeah," I said, slightly dazed. "You're so beautiful."

I didn't even notice my feet moving until we were inches apart from each other.

"You're so gorgeous, Kathleen," Olivia whispered. She moved closer to me and placed her hand on my shoulder.

My face moved closer and closer to hers. "Fuck, you're so sexy, *Angel*," I whispered back to her. I looked into her eyes, worried about her reaction to the sudden nickname.

Olivia shivered, and her arms slid around my neck as the evening breeze picked up.

I wrapped my arms around her waist.

"Is that my nickname?" she asked, but before I could answer, her mouth was so close to mine I could taste her already. "Kiss me, please," she begged.

Our lips met, warm and needy. I kissed her slowly and passionately, the tastes of both of our drinks mingling, and her tongue urged into my mouth. My tongue danced against hers. Every inch of my body wanted her, needed her. I didn't care about dinner.

My hands slid to her ass and tightly cupped her round behind. I felt her fingers slide up my neck and curl into the hair at the base of my neck. I moaned softly and gripped her tighter, eliciting a whine of pleasure from Olivia.

"I want you," I breathed against her lips.

"Take me," Olivia replied, pushing her body tighter to mine.

A shiver ran up my back. I pulled away from her just long enough to look for someplace that wasn't entirely out in the open. I gently grabbed her hand and pulled her over to a patch of grass that was halfway concealed by shrubbery and trees.

Before I could pull her back to me, Olivia was pulling me to the ground and climbing into my lap. I huffed as my fat ass hit the grass.

"Kathleen," she moaned as she straddled my lap and kissed me.

I ardently returned her kiss and ran a hand up the back of her shirt, feeling for a hook or tie. I pulled at the ribbon of her bikini top and felt it pull loose.

"I want to see you." I slid her tank top off, and her strapless top fell between us. My eyes took in her soft, natural breasts and her dark pink nipples.

"Fuck, you're beautiful; so—" The second "beautiful" was cut off as I leaned down and took one of her nipples into my mouth.

Olivia moaned and tilted her head back. I could feel the ends of her hair brush against my knees.

I swirled my tongue along her hard nipple and lost myself in the taste of her skin. It had been so long since I'd touched a woman, and I wanted to remember every moment.

Olivia ground against my lap and nudged my head with her face. I lifted my head up and eagerly claimed her mouth. In the humid island night, it was a flurry of hands and feet as I pulled her shorts and bikini bottoms down, tossing them to the grass beside us as Olivia undid my top. My heavy breasts drooped down from their perkier state, and I felt a rush of insecurity cross over me.

Until I saw the heated look in Olivia's eyes, and she rushed my lips with her own. I laid back on the grass as her fingers shimmied my own bottoms off.

Her naked body pressed to mine, and she straddled one of my thighs. I could feel her wet pussy against my skin, and I groaned into her mouth, pushing my thigh against her, rocking my own hips upward, desperate to please her.

"Oh, yes," Olivia moaned.

The sound was perfect.

Her thigh shifted to press against my own hot arousal, and I shivered.

"Yes, that's it," I gasped.

Olivia's breasts pressed to mine, and she rolled her hips harder against me.

I struggled to keep my moans soft and quiet to avoid detection.

"Yes, fuck..." Olivia whined against my lips.

I needed to taste her.

"On my face," I said, my breath but a pant.

Olivia wasted no time sliding up to straddle my face. I claimed her pussy with my mouth, going directly for her clit. Tightly gripping her hips, I swirled my tongue around the hard, throbbing nub.

Olivia's hips rolled against my face. "Please, don't stop."

I took in a breath for a split second and whispered, "I'm just getting started."

3

Olivia

I can't believe this is happening. Sure, I'd daydreamed about hooking up with a delicious stranger during my vacation, but when I'd rolled out of bed and headed to the beach, it had been the last thing on my mind.

Now I was riding an older woman's face while she ate my pussy like it was her first meal in years.

"Oh, fuck me," I moaned, trying to keep my voice down. We were mostly hidden in some plants, but there were still several angles at which someone could easily see us if they were close enough.

As Kathleen's tongue buried itself inside of my hot cunt, though, I found that, frankly, I didn't care. Let people see us. My hips rocked desperately against her face, and I tightened my thighs against the side of her face. The feeling of her hands gripping my ass and thighs drove me even more wild. Her nails bit into my flesh oh-so-perfectly.

"Yes, yes!" I tossed my head back and clamped my teeth down on my bottom lip.

I could feel my orgasm building up inside me. More powerful than it had been earlier when I'd rubbed myself to sleep.

Kathleen's mouth moved from my arousal for just a moment to demand, "Come for me, *Angel*."

That nickname from a woman I barely knew, along with her order, sent me over the edge. I gasped out in pleasure as the waves of my orgasm shivered down my thighs. My pussy tightened for a moment, sending a tingle up my clit all the way to my belly button.

"Fuck, fuck."

I panted for breath as my body went rigid, and suddenly I couldn't breathe at all. I nearly tipped backward, but Kathleen's hands held me tighter. I shivered hard as I came down from coming, my body relaxing, and I took a deep breath. Just as I was about to climb off her and dive between her legs, my mouth salivating just thinking about it, I heard something to the left of us.

"Shit," I gasped.

Laughter from what seemed to be a small group was close enough that it made my hair stand on end with anxiety.

"Oh fuck," I rolled off Kathleen and rushed for my clothing on the ground.

"Damnit." Kathleen laughed.

I looked at her with a "what are you doing?" look on my face as I struggled to pull on my shorts. It was a waste trying to find my panties. I grabbed my purse.

"Get up!" I insisted and grabbed her hand to help her up.

She seemed to finally grasp the situation and grabbed her own clothing.

"Hey, what's that?" one of the not-so-distant voices said.

I turned to look and found a pair of old eyes on my bare tits.

"Ah!" I yelped.

Before I could do anything else, Kathleen was wrapping her arm around me and towing me along as she rushed away from the scene and away from the beach.

"It's okay; I got you," she panted.

My entire face and body were hot, and I wasn't sure if it was from embarrassment, sex, or just the beach. I glanced at Kathleen long enough to see she'd got all of her own clothing on, but her bikini top was upside down, making her breasts push out the sides a bit more than usual.

My hand flew to my mouth, and I giggled. "Oh, my god!" I couldn't stop giggling. "We were almost..."

Kathleen smiled at me, then looked to the side. "You'd better get your top on, honey." She moved to stand between me and the trail back to the hotel that was a few yards away.

My face flushed deeper again, and I quickly put on my tank top, holding my bikini top in my hand because I didn't want to bother with the ties.

"Okay, I'm good," I insisted.

Kathleen turned around to look at me, her eyes darting first to my chest, then back up to my face. I noticed now that her chin was still dripping with my juices and my knees felt weak.

"Come to my hotel room?" I asked her.

Her eyes heated. "Yes, please."

I grabbed her by the hand, and now I was leading her back to the hotel.

I paid no attention to who was in the lobby when we arrived, nor if anyone was watching us hold hands as I led her to the elevator. As we got into the empty elevator and the doors closed behind us, I was suddenly shoved against the wall. My breath was pushed out of my lungs, and before I could catch it, Kathleen's lips were against mine. I moaned into her mouth and wrapped my arms around her neck. Of anyone I had ever hooked up with, Kathleen was by far the most passionate.

"God, you're so..." she mumbled into the kiss, but I couldn't make out the last word.

Whatever it was, the tone of her voice melted me. "You make me so wet," I breathed.

"I want to taste you all night." Kathleen's voice was husky and needy.

I shivered and kissed her deeply. My tongue brushed against her lower lip, asking for entrance, and was met by her tongue swirling around my own. My left leg curled up and my knee pressed to her hip. But just as I was about to pull her tighter against me, the elevator doors opened with a ding.

Kathleen pulled away from me and chuckled. "Lead the way," she insisted.

I blinked; I didn't even remember pushing the button for my floor, but there we were. I took several deep breaths and stepped out of the elevator while pulling my keycard out of my purse. "It's just a few doors down," I told her.

"Mhm," Kathleen hummed.

When I looked at her, she was just gazing at me hungrily.

I wasn't sure how old she was, but I could guess forty, at least. I realized in that moment everything I had ever been told about women over forty was wrong. Kathleen was vibrant, sexy, and sure as fuck wanted me every bit as I wanted her, if not more.

I couldn't contain my excitement as I led her to my room, smiling every step of the way. I didn't know if I'd ever see her again after that night, but I knew it was going to be a good one.

"Here we are." I opened the door, waved Kathleen inside, then closed the door as I stepped in after her.

There was no awkward small talk about the room: how nice it was or how I liked it. None of that.

Once the dim light was on, Kathleen and I kicked our sandals off, then she grabbed my waist. She licked her lips, clearly ready to taste me again, but I turned us so that she was closest to the bed.

"It's my turn to taste you," I whispered.

Our clothing quickly found its home on the floor as my lips met hers and we shuffled toward the bed. There was no time to care about who undressed who. All I wanted was to please the beautiful woman who only hours before I'd been annoyed with.

I slid between Kathleen's legs after she laid back on the bed, my eyes gliding up her soft, plush, naked body and to her light green eyes, which were filled with desire. With my pulse racing, I spread her thighs further apart and leaned my head back, trailing soft, slow kisses up from her thigh to the curve of her mound. I could feel her shiver beneath my touch as I dipped my tongue into her folds and found her clit. I wrapped my arms around her thighs and pulled myself tighter against her, my tongue swirling and lapping at her pussy.

"Fuck, you taste so good," I moaned.

I gripped Kathleen's thighs tighter as her hips rocked against my face.

"Ohhh, yes, don't stop," she moaned. Her voice was louder than it'd been on the beach, and I wanted to hear even more.

My tongue moved quicker and rougher around her clit, sliding over it every now and again. Each time my tongue flicked against her clit in an erratic rhythm, Kathleen's gasping moans filled my ears like music.

"That's it," I coaxed her.

I brought my lips around her clit and sucked as I swirled my tongue. Her juices filled my mouth and dripped down my chin onto the bed. I moaned into her pussy, mirroring her own sounds of pleasure.

"Oh, fuck, I'm coming!" Kathleen moaned louder.

I felt her body twitch and tense as I plunged my tongue into her slit, her juices flooding my senses. Her hips rocked hard against me, her thighs tugging at my arms, but I kept my grip on her.

I panted for breath as I felt her body shiver in delight, then relax, over and over until she was quiet and simply catching her breath.

I leaned my face against her thigh and licked my lips.

"Mm," I hummed out. My head was dizzy.

I laid like this for a long moment before I finally crawled up her body and laid on my side beside her.

Kathleen's eyes were half open as she looked at me. Her hand reached between us, grabbed my hip, and tugged me closer.

Before I could say anything, she was kissing me, and I eagerly kissed her back.

The smell of our arousal mixed into one intoxicating scent that wrapped around us in the humid room.

I knew I could likely continue if Kathleen wanted to, but I was perfectly comfortable as her mouth broke from mine and her head tucked near my neck.

I mimicked her sigh of delight, and we laid there until the room was colder.

My mouth was dry, and as I realized this, my stomach growled angrily. I had totally forgotten about dinner.

"You want some water?" I asked.

"I'd love some."

I reluctantly pulled myself from her embrace and grabbed two waters from the mini fridge and two granola bars from my purse that had doubled as a carry-on. Then I flopped back down on the bed and laughed affectionately as Kathleen's body jiggled.

"Sorry, here you go." I handed her the water and the snack. "I figured you'd be hungry, too."

"Thank you." She opened the water first after sitting up.

After I downed almost the entire bottle, I moved to lie on my stomach.

Things didn't feel awkward even though we'd just met. The last time I'd hooked up, it had been with a guy named Deke, and we'd just stared at each other after until I left.

For a couple minutes, there were no sounds except glugging water and crinkling wrappers.

"So, tell me more about yourself while we snack," Kathleen said. "If you'd like to, of course." She paused for a moment. "I can always leave; I don't want to overstay my welcome."

I chuckled. "You're okay," I insisted. "Uh, well, it's nothing exciting, really. I'm a waitress in Ohio. I have a cat named Grape..."

Kathleen laughed. "Grape?! That's adorable."

I grinned, and my heart fluttered, thinking about my fluffy guy. "Yeah, he's this blueish shade of gray that looks purple in the sunlight," I said with a sigh. "What about you?" I asked, "you said you're a lawyer?"

Kathleen finished chewing her mouthful. "I work at a law firm in New York City," she explained.

My heart jumped into my throat. "Wow, we're...definitely in two different worlds."

Kathleen nodded slowly, and I wondered if she was thinking the same thing I was.

"This was really nice," I smiled softly.

"...But?" she prodded.

I pursed my lips. "Well, I'd like to see you again, but..."

Kathleen eyed me and tilted her head to the side. "Our lives are probably too different for this to continue outside of St. Lucia," she said, all but reading my mind.

I nodded and shrugged my shoulders.

"I'm up for a 'no strings attached' hook-up for the rest of your vacation," Kathleen told me.

My face flushed, and I chewed on my lip. "Really?"

She smirked at me and brushed her curls behind her shoulder, leaning closer.

"As long as I get to see you again."

I swallowed. "Okay," I said. "No feelings. Just enjoying each other's company."

"Just pleasure." Kathleen nodded, and her gaze became heated again.

I shivered.

"Unfortunately, I need to get going. I'm already late for dinner with my co-workers." She sighed. "I'd invite you, but..."

I shook my head. "That's okay."

My eyes followed her as Kathleen got out of bed and disappeared into the bathroom. After the sink turned off, she came out dressed and headed for the door.

There was no goodbye kiss, just a soft smile and a wave before she left.

I sighed and laid back on the bed.

"Fuck," I mumbled.

I squeezed my thighs closed and chewed at my lip as I thought about Kathleen. There was no doubt in my mind that I wanted to fuck her again, but more than that, I wanted to see her again.

No feelings, I reminded myself.

"Ah, shit!" I gasped and sat up in bed.

We didn't trade numbers!

4

Kathleen

I'd missed dinner with Robert, Liam and Christa, but that didn't stop me from stopping to get myself something to eat while I prepared to deal with their questions when I got back to the hotel room.

I was still riding the high from sex with Olivia. *Fuck, maybe I should've just stayed the night.* The rush of clarity after our tryst, however, had gotten me thinking I should at least try to meet up with my coworkers for dinner, and the next thing I knew, I was gone.

I realized only once I was messaging Robert while in the elevator that I hadn't given Olivia my number, and she hadn't given me hers.

Ah, well.

I knew where her room was; I'd put it down in my Notes app, so I wasn't concerned. I'd just knock on her door tomorrow and get her number so we could figure out plans to hook up again.

I was blushing as I headed back to the hotel room. My stomach was full of grilled chicken and fries, and I felt more satisfied than I had in years. In several ways.

I debated going back to Olivia's room now, spending the night with her, but I decided she probably had other things to be doing. She was twenty-seven, after all. She probably had a party to attend.

All I wanted to do was lounge on the patio and read.

"Couldn't make it to dinner?" Liam asked sarcastically the second I was in the hotel room.

I rolled my eyes and pulled my phone out to put it on the charger. "We have two weeks here," I reminded him. "I'm sure we'll be tired of the restaurant by the time we leave."

Christa was sitting on the small couch, flipping through a magazine with shirtless men on the cover. She looked up at Liam and shrugged. "Kathy's right; I didn't think it was a big deal," she said, then frowned at me. "You could have let us know before, though."

"I'm sorry, something suddenly came up," I said. I didn't really want to talk about my sex life with them.

"Like what?" Robert asked from his bed.

"Beach stuff."

They all looked at me silently. Waiting.

"Fine, if you must know, I was getting railed," I said.

"Oh, jeez." Robert crinkled his nose.

Liam was narrowing his eyes like he was trying to imagine that.

"Oh gosh, that's...a little...inappropriate." Christa chuckled weakly.

"Hey, you asked." I put my hands up, then grabbed my bag from the end of the bed to get my pajamas on. "Anyway, we need to figure out the sleeping situation," I insisted.

"Why don't you just stay with your 'fuck buddy'?" Liam asked.

I nearly growled but kept calm and took a deep breath. "Maybe I will, but not tonight," I replied. "Now, beds, figure. It. Out."

⚡

Fuck me, that was forty minutes of absolute bullshit. In the end, Liam and Robert finally got over their toxic masculinity issues and agreed to share a bed, but Christa really didn't want to share a bed with me. I can't lie; it kind of hurt how much she protested against it, but I decided not to argue with her.

So, I took the couch.

It had been years since I'd slept on a couch. They couldn't at least make it a pull-out bed?

After a couple hours of reading, I laid on the couch under a thin blanket, staring at the ceiling while listening to snoring. I could imagine Olivia wandering into some sweaty beach house party and dancing. I wondered if she'd hook up with anyone else.

I tried to convince myself that I was only thinking about it because I'd forgotten to make sure we were both "safe," so to speak.

Before I could think about it too hard, I was dozing off.

In the morning, Christa insisted we all go to breakfast togeth-er. I was starving when I woke up, so that was fine with me. After a shower, I coaxed my freshly washed and dried curls into an up-do and pulled on a long, flowing floral dress.

Most of the way to the restaurant was smooth planks in the sand, and Robert had no real issue managing unless he strayed off of them. The ramp to the entrance of the restaurant, however, was much steeper than he was used to, so I helped him up while Liam and Christa got our table.

"I'm going to talk to the manager about this ramp after breakfast," I told him.

"Oh, no! You don't have to do that, Kathy," he told me.

I opened the door so he could wheel in. "Are you going to?" I asked.

"Nah, I'm probably the only person in a wheelchair that's been here in months."

I stepped in behind him. "Well, we can make it easier for the next guy," I replied, "if you're alright with that."

Robert smiled bashfully at me and then led me to the table Liam and Christa were sitting at.

Before the server arrived, I went to the restroom. I was washing my hands when I looked to the side and my heart nearly jumped out of my chest in surprise.

"Olivia." I coughed and pulled myself together. "You're here?" I shook my head and continued drying my hands. "Of course you're here, sorry; I just wasn't expecting to see you."

"Oh, Kathleen!" Olivia said, her face bright red, "I decided to get some breakfast. I'm not normally awake so early, but I forgot dinner last night, and I'm starving."

Damnit. I should've gone back last night.

Ignoring my thought, I chuckled softly. "Well, at least you weren't following me." I teased her.

Olivia's face grew darker. "Oh, fuck. No!" she gasped. "I mean, I was hoping I'd run into you because I realized we forgot to trade numbers last night, and I went out into the hallway looking for you, but I think you were already in the elevator..."

She was rambling, but I didn't mind it at all. Or the way she shifted on her feet, embarrassed, and fidgeted with several locks of her mousy blonde hair. She looked so damn cute; I couldn't stand it.

"Hey, it's alright," I insisted, stepping closer to her. "I know where your room is, anyway. I was planning on seeing if you were in later and sliding my number under your door if not."

I lifted a hand and brushed her hair behind her ear.

Olivia chewed on her bottom lip, and it drove me wild. I didn't care about breakfast at that moment, even if my stomach was aching with hunger. There was a different hunger I was more concerned with.

"Oh," Olivia mumbled, "right. I'm silly." She shook her head.

She moved closer to me in the tile-walled bathroom. There were two stalls, and no one else in the room. It was just us.

"You are anything but silly," I told her, voice quiet. I could hear the flirty edge in my own voice, and I watched the way Olivia's own mannerisms shifted in interest.

"Oh, yeah?" she asked.

"Mhm." I stepped closer and closer, until Olivia's back pressed against the wall beside the light switch.

"Maybe I was looking for you." Olivia smiled at me, her own tone teasing.

I couldn't hold myself back any longer. My hands reached for her hips as I leaned forward and kissed her. The sweet and salty scent of her skin overwhelmed me as she kissed me back.

Olivia's arms wrapped around my neck and pulled my plush body tighter against her curvy one.

She moaned into the kiss as my lips ardently claimed hers and my fingers gripped her hips tighter.

I wasn't sure how I was ever going to get anything else done on vacation as long as she was nearby, but I found I didn't mind that idea. This beautiful young woman that was a distraction from the shitty work I eventually had to go back to? I'd take it. I'd take her, happily. Over and over.

Just as Olivia's fingers were curling against the nape of my neck, the bathroom door opened, and I heard a soft, familiar gasp.

"Oh, gosh, sorry."

I reluctantly pulled away from Olivia, just in time to see Christa's slender behind rushing into a stall.

My face flushed slightly, but it was nowhere near as red as Olivia's was.

"Oh God," Olivia said, cringing.

I chuckled softly. "I suppose I should let you get to breakfast," I said huskily.

Olivia shivered. "Mm, yeah." She sighed and pulled her phone out of her purse. "Here," she offered it to me after swiping at the screen.

I didn't have my bag with my phone with me, so giving her my number would have to do. Taking the phone from her, I quickly put my name and number in her contacts and handed it back.

"Thanks," Olivia murmured. She put her phone away and looked me in the eye one last time.

It looked like she was going to say something else, but her eyes darted behind me toward the stalls.

"See you," I said, giving her permission to disengage from our...conversation.

She smiled and nodded before moving around me toward the other stall.

I shook my head and left the restroom, still tasting Olivia on my lips.

Olivia Waitts: *I'll be there in five*

Me: *No rush. I'm waiting outside.*

I shoved my phone back into my bag and brushed a loose curl of my hair away from my eyes. My hair was still in the up-do, but I'd pulled some curls out to frame my face. I had also adjusted the neckline of my flowing dress to be more revealing and cinched the waist ever so slightly.

Olivia and I were just hooking up while on vacation, but I still wanted to look good.

I was about to pull my phone out one more time when I heard Olivia's voice from a few yards away. "Hey!" she called, "I'm a few minutes late; I realized halfway here that I totally forgot to put my card back in my purse."

I smirked at her. "You didn't need to stop for that," I insisted. "This is on me."

Olivia's face widened in surprise. "Oh, wow, thank you."

I wasn't going to say it out loud, but I assumed I had more money than she did, even if I wasn't happy about not being given a food budget for the trip.

"You look shocked," I said, reaching my hand out to her.

"Well, we're just hooking up; I didn't expect...going out to dinner," Olivia admitted.

I frowned briefly. Who had she hooked up with before that hadn't ever even taken her for dinner? Perhaps my generation's idea of hook-up etiquette was out of date. I cringed inwardly.

Then I quickly put a soft smile on my face. "I'd like to feed you before I fuck you, darling." I wiggled the fingers of my outstretched hand.

Olivia's neck went red, and she brushed her beautiful hair behind her ears before finally taking my hand. "I'd love that." Her seductive tone told me she meant both.

I ushered her into the restaurant, and the hostess quickly led us both to a booth in the back of the restaurant, per my request.

The light dangling above us was dim, and a cluster of tea candles rested in the center of the round table. The booth was a half-circle. I'd been worried at first about sitting comfortably in it due to my size, but I was delighted to be able to slide in with ease.

Olivia seemed to teeter on her short heels as she thought about where to sit exactly.

"Come here," I said to her, patting the spot next to me.

44

She smiled and slid in beside me, leaving just enough space that we wouldn't elbow each other while dining.

"Your server will be right with you," the hostess said as she placed our menus on the table.

Not a second after the hostess left did the server step over to our table and place two waters with straws in front of us. I glanced at their name tag.

"Hi, I'm Xav, and I'll be your server tonight. Can I get you anything else to drink while you decide?"

"No, thank you," I told them and looked at Olivia.

"I'll have a Diet Coke, please."

"Right on it; you two take your time."

Once Xav was gone, I glanced down at my menu, which was chock-full of sea food options and delicious sides. It didn't take me long to decide what I wanted.

"I really want this, but what you picked sounds good too," Olivia said. Her brow was knit.

I clicked my tongue. "Why don't we share?" I asked.

"That's a great idea." She smiled and closed her menu, then opened it again a second later, blinking like she'd already forgotten what she had wanted.

After Xav got our order put in, we were left all alone. There were others in the restaurant, but most of them were closer to the front.

"I'm surprised you didn't pick a seat with an ocean view," Olivia said as she sipped at her soda.

I scooted closer to her. "Oh, that was for a very good reason."

She tilted her head to the side and raised a brow. "Oh, really?"

I looked to see if anyone was headed our way before my eyes met hers again. "I'll show you," I told her, lowering my voice.

My hand slipped under the table and crept underneath the hem of her sun dress, and my fingers slid along her warm thigh.

"Oh." Olivia gasped softly.

"Is this alright?" I asked, keeping my eyes on her, watching her throat move as she swallowed. "Yes," she said, her voice breathy.

I caressed her soft skin with my fingers and gently nudged at her thighs. "Open your legs for me," I coaxed.

Olivia did as she was told, and my hand slid between those delicious thighs of hers to the even more succulent dessert of her pussy. As my fingers met her bare, hot, and wet labia, I realized she wasn't wearing any panties.

"Mm, no panties. What a naughty girl," I purred.

Olivia shivered. "I want to be a good girl," she insisted, her voice nearly a whine.

I wasn't usually big into power dynamics, but in that moment, there was nothing hotter than the way Olivia was submitting to me.

"Well, you can be a good girl and cum for me," I whispered.

I quickly looked away from her again just to make sure there were still no prying eyes. I hadn't seen any cameras in the back, either, so I was sure we'd be good.

My index and middle fingers collected her juices and slowly slid into her pussy. Olivia bit her bottom lip hard, and in the desperate look in her eyes, I saw the moan she was aching to release. I knew we only had a couple minutes at most; the food we had ordered wouldn't take long to cook or prepare. As my fingers pumped in and out of Olivia, she turned her head away from me slightly, her eyes closed.

I placed a finger on her cheek with my free hand and turned her face back to me. "Don't look away; I want to see your face when you cum, *Angel*."

Fuck, that nickname. I knew it was going to get me in trouble; I could already feel the attachment forming, but I brushed it off.

My fingers curled up, and the tips brushed the section of her clit that was inside of her walls as I thrust them again and again. Olivia squirmed against my hand in her seat, her face going pink as she struggled not to moan out loud.

"That's it." I moved my fingers faster. "Come for me."

I could smell freshly cooked food from a distance.

"Oh, fuck..." Olivia whispered and then buried her face in my shoulder.

I gasped as I felt her teeth clamp down into my flesh, making my own pussy throb. Her body went rigid, and her walls squeezed against my fingers. Her juices soaked into the hem of her dress and dripped onto the seating of the booth.

"Good girl," I whispered into her ear.

Olivia relaxed and leaned off of me just as Xav was rounding the corner. Her teeth had granted me freedom, but I could still feel the sting.

I pulled my fingers out of her and brought them to my mouth, sucking her juices off of my fingers. "Mm," I hummed out.

I quickly opened wet napkins from the table and helped Olivia clean the seat between her thighs. She adjusted her dress in a panic, and I hid the used napkins in my bag as Xav placed our food on the table.

The air smelled like sex, but if they noticed, they didn't say anything besides, "Enjoy! And let me know if you need anything else."

"We sure will," I told them.

Olivia was too busy trying not to look like she was panting, but her red face and the sweat beaded on her forehead gave her away.

"They're going to get a big tip," I mumbled.

Olivia chuckled as Xav disappeared, and she finally took a deep breath.

"That was..." She sighed, looking dizzy. Then she licked at her lips. "I should help you," she whispered.

My thighs squeezed together. I was very wet, but the food in front of us was hot, and...ugh. "I'd love that, but I did promise I would feed you, and I have to meet my coworkers for an hour or two after this," I reminded her.

Olivia frowned. "Right." She sucked down almost all of her soda before speaking again. "But, later?"

I eyed her hungrily. "Later, most definitely."

Olivia smiled and started to dig into her food.

"So, I take it you've never been to St. Lucia before?" I asked.

She shook her head. "Hell no; I've never been on any vacation outside of the states before."

I nodded and took a bite of my own food. "That's a shame."

"Well, it took me three years to save for this one."

I coughed. "Wow," I mumbled. "I mean, that makes sense."

Olivia giggled but didn't say anything.

The sound made me weak.

5

Olivia

Halfway through my meal, I still felt flustered. It was very difficult to focus on my food when my thighs were still pulsing. Somehow, I managed.

"Splitting was really a good idea," I said.

Kathleen nodded as she chewed and swallowed. "It really was. We get the best of both dishes." She smiled.

I smiled back at her. My nose and ears were hot as I remembered the way she'd sucked my juices off her fingers earlier. "Yeah. I think I prefer the sauce on this one though," I insisted as I took another bite.

"Hmm." Kathleen tapped her finger on the rim of her glass. "Me too."

It was strange for me, having small talk and dinner with a hookup. I couldn't remember the last time someone I'd hooked up with even offered to make me breakfast. I'd offered a few people a meal if we'd ended up at my apartment, but most of the time they'd already left.

Now that I thought about it, I realized I had never had a true "no strings" agreement before. Just some hookups I'd see once or twice before never hearing from them again.

"So, do you take all of your hookups to dinner?" I asked. I tried to act like I was teasing, but I really wanted to know more about Kathleen's sex and—dare I say—dating life.

She raised a brow. "How many do you think I have?" She took another bite of food in a slow and amused manner, plucking the food off the end of the fork with a flick of her wrist.

"Um..." I pursed my lips, about to answer her question.

"I'm kidding," she replied. "No. I don't hook up very often, actually."

I blinked, surprised, and tried to keep my tone casual. "Really?"

"Do you?" Kathleen reversed my question.

"Well, I used to. The last year or so of work, I haven't had sex at all until...well, now." I bit my lip and ignored how much I wanted to give Kathleen the pleasure she'd given me in this booth.

"Hmm. Well, we probably should have spoken about this beforehand, I realize that, but I'm negative for everything," Kathleen told me.

It took me a moment to realize what she meant, and I swallowed the large gulp of Diet Coke I had in my mouth. "Me too," I told her. "I would've told you before anything happened if...yeah." I chuckled weakly.

Kathleen nodded. "I just want to be open." A moment later, a slightly crooked smirk appeared on her face.

"What?" I asked.

"You're going to be very open tonight."

I giggled and nudged her with my shoulder. "You are," I mumbled, squeezing my thighs tighter together.

We both continued eating until we were done and asked for to-go boxes, which Kathleen insisted I take with me. But we didn't need to leave just yet.

"How about desert?" I asked.

Kathleen licked her lips. "Mm, I'm not sure I have time, but we can do dessert when we meet up again later?"

"I'd like that." I scooted closer to her.

I wasn't sure what the rules were with "no strings," especially not in this strange situation where we were out to dinner together, all but cuddling in a booth. I understood the main point, however: no getting attached and no expectations of seeing each other again once my vacation was over.

"So, no sex in a year and a half?" Kathleen asked.

I shook my head. "You?"

"Two and a half years," she replied.

I chewed on my lip for a moment, thinking. "My last time was with...an ex-friend. He told me he was moving to another country. I thought I wouldn't see him again for years, and we both wanted to know what it was like. Everyone always thought we were fucking anyway." I chuckled, then my face fell. "Turns out he was lying. He was just moving to another state to be with a girl he met a few months before who didn't like the sound of me."

My eyes met Kathleen's, and I saw aggravation there and realized I might have over-shared.

"I-I'm sorry; it just kind of spilled out of me," I mumbled and scooted away from her.

"No! You're fine; you have a life. I'm pissed off at that douchebag for you, and I don't even know him." She huffed angrily and finished her water.

I laughed softly. "The really sad part is the girl found out, but decided to stay with him anyway—making it all my fault, even though I didn't know about her—and now they're married."

"Fuck me." Kathleen sighed. "That's rough."

I nodded.

It was silent for a moment. "I've been divorced two years," she said.

"Oh?" I asked, prompting her for more.

"Yeah." With another sigh, she settled further into the seat. "We started dating when we were teenagers but broke things off before college. She got in touch with me about...oh, over ten years ago. We were friends for a while, ended up dating for two years, married for five." She exhaled, lips vibrating, and I could tell it was a difficult topic for her.

"Why didn't it work out? If I can ask..." I backtracked slightly.

Kathleen's head bobbled as she seemed to think about how to answer that. "Short or long answer?" she asked.

"Both. Short first."

"We were unfaithful to each other." Kathleen looked wary as she said this.

My heart jumped into my throat, and I felt a wave of anxiety cross over me, but I pushed it down. "Okay," I replied, fiddling with a straw wrapper to keep myself level. "Long answer."

"My ex-wife, Lauralee, she wanted to recapture the past, and I wanted to move on. She was still terrified about what people in our home town thought, and, well, I didn't give her enough compassion about it. I wanted her to just get over it." She looked genuinely regretful. "We were well matched in chemistry, but we couldn't talk about the hard stuff."

I folded my arms under my breasts, trying to take everything in with a rational mind.

"So, good in bed, bad in communication?" I asked.

Kathleen laughed weakly. "Yes, you could say that." She turned her body more toward mine. "We both had issues, with ourselves and each other. Both of us looked for help from other people. We broke up about five years ago, but we still saw each other casually on and off and didn't get officially divorced until two years ago," Kathleen explained.

"You never tried to work it out again?" I asked, curious.

"No. I've been in therapy for three years and...so has she. We're just not the same people anymore, but in a good way." Her smile was bittersweet. "I regret the choices I made with her, and I've vowed to myself to never make them again with anyone else, but I've moved on."

I swallowed. "Wow."

"I've laid a lot on you, haven't I?"

Exhaling, I tried to say no but ended up nodding my head. "A little, but, you know, honesty is hard to get sometimes. I appreciate it."

Kathleen smiled at me. "Well, we're never going to see each other again after this week, right? Why waste time skirting the hard subjects?"

There went my stomach and heart again. "Yeah, you're right." I forced a chuckle.

This is fine.

After dinner, I decided to go off on my own while Kathleen met up with her coworkers. I'd now spent most my vacation fucking, and I really wanted to go for a swim. It was nearly dark, but that was the best time to swim from what I'd gathered. It wasn't too hot, the water was perfect, and most of the other vacation-goers were back at their hotels.

I slipped into the cool water in my bikini, my hair tied in a messy bun, and sighed. When the water was at my waist, I stopped and waved my arms around under the gently lapping waves. The sun was just disappearing over the horizon, and the moon was clearly visible in the sky. The mix of dark blue, purple, and orange was stunning, and I found myself staring at the sunset for several minutes until the sun had completely disappeared.

"Wow!" I said with awe.

I was startled by the sound of a couple screaming with laughter several yards away as they splashed each other. I chuckled and continued further into the water, swimming and floating until about half an hour later, when I found myself alone. And lonely. Before taking my leave from the ocean, I walked in the shallows for a moment, then made my way off the beach.

After rinsing my feet in the small shower, I grabbed my beach bag and decided to go looking for my bikini bottoms in the grassy area where Kathleen and I had been the night before. I used the flashlight on my phone to get a better look at the grass and brush.

"Ah!" I bent down and plucked the sting bikini panties off the ground and held them in the air. I doubted anyone had disturbed them, but I was still wary. I slid them into the empty side pocket of my bag and looked around, thankful that the coast was clear. Thinking about my time with Kathleen made my knees weak. God, I'd spent more time having sex in public—and almost getting caught!—in the last two days than I had in my entire life. And I had to admit, I kind of liked it—the high of the pleasure.

My phone was still in my hand. I chewed on my bottom lip and turned off the flashlight. Then, I sunk down onto the grass and swiped to my camera, turning on the front facing illumination. My pulse quickened just thinking about it, and as my hand slid down into my bikini, it only grew heavier.

My fingers brushed over my clit, and I pushed the record button. Tilting my head back as I caressed my wet pussy, I relived the memory of Kathleen's fingers sliding between my thighs at the restaurant and moaned softly.

"Oh, yes."

My hips rocked against my hand as I rubbed myself, and it was so hard not to bring myself over the edge. But I so desperately wanted Kathleen to be the one to do that later, so I forced myself to stop. I shivered as I pulled my hand out of my bikini bottoms and stopped recording, using the grass to wipe my fingers off.

I pushed up off the ground and checked what the signal was like. The Wi-Fi from the hotel was just barely there. I walked a few yards further from the beach until I could send the twenty-second video to Kathleen, and I giggled softly.

"Let's see what she thinks about that." I squirmed slightly, still wet, then fixed my bag over my shoulder and headed back to the hotel.

I felt giddy as I walked, even if I was still incredibly turned on and had no idea when Kathleen would be available. The entrance to the hotel was only a few yards away when I heard shuffling steps behind me, then a voice.

"Hey, baby," he said.

My shoulders tensed, and even though I knew I should just keep walking, my feet stopped in their tracks. I turned to check that he was talking to me, and not some other girl out in the night. Sure enough, this man, maybe in his late twenties or early thirties, wearing a floral shirt was looking right at me.

"You wanna get a drink?" he asked, without me having said anything.

"No, thanks," I replied, turning away from him.

"Oh, really?" he scoffed. "I saw you out there; you looked pretty interested."

My face flushed deeply, and I stuttered out a reply as I took a stop closer to the hotel. "I'm n-not."

A firm hand grabbed my wrist, and I was tugged back. I gasped and quickly yanked my body away from him, but he maintained his hold on my wrist.

"Hey!" I squeezed my hand in a fist, flexing my arm and pulling harder. "Let go of me!"

He seemed concerned about the volume of my voice and let go of my wrist. "You're the one jerkin' it on the beach, lady!" he huffed.

My entire body was covered in goosebumps despite the warm air.

Just as was about to step away from him, I heard another voice. "Excuse me, what's going on here?" Kathleen asked sharply. With so much rage in her eyes, I had no doubt that she'd seen him grab me.

"Nothing that concerns you," he growled.

Kathleen was suddenly standing between us. "If you touch her—actually, no," she growled at him. "If you talk to her—or even look at her—again, you'll be leaving here without your hands and needing a damn good lawyer. Do you understand me?" In her anger, Kathleen looked taller, and her nostrils flared.

"Jesus, got it!" The man put his hands up and backed away.

Kathleen turned to me, her brow furrowed but her features softened. "Are you okay?" she asked.

I nodded. "I'm fine."

"You're shaking like a leaf," Kathleen said as she reached and brushed her fingers along my arm.

I hadn't realized it, but she was right. Not only that, but all arousal I'd been previously feeling had been sucked from my body. Folding my arms, I assured her, "I'll be fine."

"Come on, let's get away from the hotel," she suggested. "There's an art museum about a fifteen-minute walk from here."

I just nodded and let her take my hand and lead me away from the hotel.

We didn't talk the entire walk. At first I thought maybe she didn't want to, but about halfway there, I realized she was letting me decompress, for which I was grateful. I really needed it. The steadiness of each step, the gentle breeze, and her hand in mine all worked as one to calm me down. By the time we got to Eudovic's Art Studio, I wasn't shivering anymore.

"Feeling better?" she asked.

"Yes." I sighed. "It was...probably my fault, anyway. I don't know if you got it, but I was recording a video outside, and...I think he saw."

Kathleen turned to look at me before we went inside. "I saw the video; it was...incredibly sexy. But that doesn't matter. It's not an invitation to grab you."

I swallowed hard. "Thank you." Logically, I knew that, but it was just easier to blame myself.

She seemed to read my mind and continued to hold my hand as we went inside.

I realized we were all alone there other than the woman standing near the back of the studio, smiling and waving at us. I waved back and squeezed Kathleen's hand tighter.

"It closes in twenty minutes, but I thought the walk here would help," Kathleen explained. "And it's really a beautiful collection."

I smiled softly. "The walk definitely helped."

I glanced around the open space that was filled with wooden art pieces of various sizes. My eyes landed on a mahogany piece of a curvy woman intertwined with a tree that swirled around her. The light in the room glinted off the sculpture's glossy finish.

"Oh, wow!"

I looked around in awe at the other perfectly carved pieces of art. They twisted and turned in abstract ways, and I found myself absolutely captivated.

"Vincent Joseph Eudovic uses only the wood and roots from trees on the island?" I said, mostly to myself, as I read a little plaque near one of the sculptures. "That's amazing."

Kathleen wrapped her arm around my waist and pulled me closer. "It really is."

Her arm around me made me feel more comfortable than I could ever remember feeling with anyone else. I tried to push the feeling away. It was just a hookup, nothing else.

Still, I was enjoying Kathleen's company.

"Thanks for standing up for me back there," I said, finally feeling steady enough to bring up the situation without tearing up.

"I'm sure you can handle yourself, but..." Kathleen shook her head. "I couldn't let some jackass manhandle you that way."

I smiled weakly and decided to move on from the subject. I'd simply wanted to thank her.

Knowing we only had a few minutes until we'd need to get out, I led her to another sculpture.

"So, are you big into art?" I asked, looking over at her.

Kathleen pursed her lips. "I try to be. I'm not very knowledgeable about it, but I think the value of art is beyond what most people believe and pay.."

I raised my eyebrows and chuckled.

"What?" she asked.

"It's just...most people I've hooked up with would have lied and said they're really into art and tried to pass off a story showing how much they know," I replied.

Kathleen snickered. "Well, I think it's silly to impress someone with shit you don't actually know about. Then you have to keep it up for...fuck, who knows how long?"

I laughed. "That's so true! It always falls apart."

Kathleen led me around a bit more, then I watched as she slipped some money into the tip jar that was sitting around, nearly full. Just as we were nearing the exit, I noticed that woman wrapped in a tree again, and the price below it. Apparently, some pieces were available to purchase.

"You alright?" Kathleen asked.

It was way too much money for me to spend, even though it would be worth it.

"Ah, yeah." Talking myself out of buying the sculpture, I turned away from it and let her lead me out of the small building and into the night.

"It's so peaceful out here." I looked up at the sky. The glittering stars were more visible than I'd ever seen them anywhere else.

"It really is," she replied, and we continued walking. "Are you a fan of art?" she asked. "I noticed you were a bit star-struck by some pieces."

I flushed and brushed a lock of hair behind my ear. "Not usually, but those carvings really felt...special. Like there was so much emotion and tenderness in them." I smiled softly.

Kathleen smiled back at me in the dimness, then eyed me. "You're covered in goosebumps. Here, take my cover up," she insisted. She slid it off her shoulders, revealing more of her flowing sun dress.

I stopped so she could pull it on over my head. It was quite over-sized on me, but that only made it cozier.

"You sure?" I asked, "I have a cover up in my bag. It's pretty sandy, but—"

"You're in just a bikini; I have this dress, at least." She chuckled. "No need to deal with the sand."

I tugged the fabric up closer and inhaled Kathleen's scent as we continued walking toward the hotel.

6

Kathleen

"You've been spending a lot of time with this 'Olivia,'" Christa said. She was lounging beside me on the beach, a fruity, definitely-not-virgin drink in her hand.

I took a sip of my drink and tried to ignore the accusing inflection of her tone.

"Well, that's what you do when you're hooking up on vacation," I told her. I did my best to tone down my wording with her, not wanting to hear her gasp and watch her shift uncomfortably.

"Mm, is it?" she asked.

I rolled my eyes from behind my sunglasses but said nothing else.

"She's right," Liam said as he walked over, two fresh drinks in his hands.

I scoffed. "How much of that did you even hear?"

"Just the last bit, but I'm sure she is."

I shook my head.

"Have you ever had a summer...hook-up?" Robert asked Christa, the last two words drawn out. He was sitting on the other side of Christa, much to Liam's dismay. Neither of us wanted to watch them make out on the beach.

Liam handed Robert one of the drinks and then sat in his lounge chair beside him.

"Before now," I added, side-eying Liam playfully, a soft smirk playing over my lips.

As much as I didn't want to watch them fuck, I really didn't care what they were doing with their time together. I didn't get paid enough to uphold the company dating policy; and it wasn't like the Big Guys followed it.

I looked away from them toward the sun, which was only an hour away from setting. We'd been hanging out on the beach most of the afternoon. As I was about to look back at my coworkers, I saw a familiar wave of blonde hair, heart-shaped face, and round ass from a distance. My heart thudded as I looked at Olivia, standing there in her sheer cover up over her bikini, talking happily to a tall, tan, dark-haired woman.

It had been a few days since the incident outside of the hotel. There was only one more day until Olivia would have to leave and I'd be left here for another week.

I took a slow breath, trying not to think about it as I had been...all week.

Every time we touched, kissed, and tangled up in each other. Each time we cuddled and whispered to each other afterward, spending that blissful time talking about memories and what our favorite foods were.

I knew so much more about her than I expected when we made our agreement. I had to keep reminding myself this was no feelings, just pleasure.

"Hey did you hear?" Christa asked, snapping me out of my thoughts.

I flinched and looked back at her. "Ah, yeah," I mumbled and sipped at my drink.

"So, you agree?" she asked.

I turned my head to look back at Olivia as my straw was in my mouth.

"Mhm," I hummed.

"That you clearly have feelings for Olivia?" Christa said, purposefully not including that in her first question until after I'd answered.

"Wait!" I blinked and nearly growled at her. "Don't do that!" I huffed and set my drink down on the small table between our chairs.

Christa giggled, and Liam laughed along with her.

I looked back over at Olivia, watching the woman she was talking to brush her hands along Olivia's arms, and move closer and closer to her every minute.

My ears and nose were hot. My hands balled into fists.

I am not jealous.

I had never been the jealous type.

Still, as I watched, my stomach tightened.

Maybe I needed to find someone else to hook up with instead of just Olivia. Then, I wouldn't care so much what she was doing. After all, this was just...casual.

Sure, I knew that her favorite dish is green bean casserole, her favorite color is yellow, and she binge watches cooking competitions on the weekends, but that meant nothing.

I made a sudden decision to get up and find a pretty woman to talk to while I finished my drink.

"You know, you and Liam have been attached at the hip since we got here, so you're one to talk," I shot at Christa.

She flushed and tossed a tiny umbrella in my direction. It landed a few feet short of me in the sand. I picked it up and tossed it back at her before turning away from the group.

I walked right by Olivia, forcing myself not to see if she was looking at me, and over to a woman who looked closer to my own age. She was wearing a big floppy hat and trying to get the bubble blower she was using working.

"Hi, I'm Kathleen," I said casually, waving a hand.

"Hi! Lyn." She chuckled and gave the thing another tap.

"Can't get that thing working?" I asked, tilting my head to the side and putting a hand on my hip. While she was looking down at it, I noted her appearance. Very short blonde hair, bikini top, khaki shorts...and Birkenstocks. If I had to guess, she was most likely part of the "Alphabet," so to speak.

"Not a bit," she sighed and looked up at me with stunning blue eyes.

"Can I give it a go?" I asked her. "It can be tricky."

"Oh, you betcha. Maybe you can get it workin'."

Despite my intentions, even as I flirted with Lyn, I struggled not to look at Olivia to see what she was doing.

An hour later, the sun was disappearing into the horizon, and my tongue was disappearing into Lyn's mouth.

This was strange for me, this whole vacation. I'd kissed more people in one week than I had in years: two.

Lyn seemed more than interested in me, her hands on my hips and one of my hands on hers. We leaned against the side of the grill hut and just kissed. Somehow, fiddling with the bubble blower, which I had gotten working, had turned into talking about family and that had turned into me revealing my sexuality and Lyn revealing she had never kissed a woman before, but wanted to.

"What do you think?" I whispered against her lips.

"Oh, gosh...I like it," she said, giggling.

My thighs and face were flush, but even as she kissed me again, I felt like my eyes were on the back of my head, searching for long wavy blonde hair and brown eyes.

Lyn pulled away from me. "Ya alright?"

"Ah, no." I shrugged, stepping back. "I thought making out with one beautiful woman on the beach would get my mind off another, but..." I trailed off.

Lyn blinked. "Oh! I'm sorry." She rubbed my shoulder. "Well, you gave me my first girl kiss, so it wasn't for nothin'."

I nodded. I felt no need to lie to this stranger. I could've told her I had to go meet my coworkers, or I was fine, but it frankly was no skin off my back if she got upset over the truth. Though I was grateful that she seemed to understand.

"My ex-husband is still fresh in my mind," she said, thinking she knew where my was at.

My heart jumped into my throat. "It's...not like that. At least, not quite," I insisted hurriedly.

Lyn raised an eyebrow and laughed. "Alright, whatever you say. Hope ya figure it out." She gave me a gentle wave before disappearing around the front of the hut.

I sighed and turned around to lean my back against the wall.

When I did so, I saw Olivia standing some odd yards away, holding something in her hand and looking right at me. I was about to wave when her eyebrows knit and she took a step back.

It wasn't until Olivia turned on her heel and darted away that I realized she seemed upset.

"Olivia!" I called after her.

I hurried through the sand after her, stopping abruptly as she turned around.

"Yeah?" she asked.

Her shoulders were tense, inching closer to her ears.

"Are you alright?" I asked.

She cleared her throat. "Yeah, I'm fine." Her eyes glistened, and it made my stomach ache.

"Don't lie to me," I told her. My voice was harsher than intended. I stepped closer to her.

Olivia sighed and chewed on her bottom lip for a second or two before she finally spoke.

"Fine. I saw you kissing another woman, and..." She waved a hand around. "I felt...upset. Jealous, I guess; but I have no right to be jealous. It's silly."

My ears flushed, and my stomach fluttered. "You were jealous?" I asked. I needed to hear it again, to know for sure.

Olivia's face reddened, and her brow knit deeper. "Yes! But I know our agreement. Just pleasure. Nothing about hooking up with anyone else."

I couldn't keep the words from coming out. "I was jealous, too," I admitted.

"What?" she asked, stepping closer. In her hand was a small mesh bag with something colorful inside.

"I saw you flirting with someone on the beach earlier," I explained. "And I was jealous." As we closed the distance between us, our faces only inches apart, I added, "I was jealous of the idea of you fucking someone else, of someone else touching you."

Olivia exhaled shakily, but kept her eyes locked on mine. "I was flirting with her, but I can't stop thinking about you."

"I can't stop thinking about you either, *Angel*." As I brushed my fingers along her cheek, and she tilted her head against my touch. "And I know this will never work out away from this island, but I'm not ready to say goodbye tomorrow," I whispered.

Olivia frowned and clasped my hand. "Me, either. I've had such a good time."

"Then stay," I insisted. "Stay until the end of my vacation."

Olivia's eyes widened. "I-I can't afford to—"

"I'll pay for everything. I'll even talk to the hotel about extending your room for another week. Please," I begged. I wasn't ready to say goodbye, even if I knew I'd have to, eventually.

I had never truly begged in my entire life, and here I was doing it to a veritable stranger.

Olivia blushed harder, then jumped slightly on her tiptoes. "Ah! Okay!" she squealed.

I grinned and wrapped my arms around her, pulling her tight to me. She tossed her arms around my neck. Her mouth captured mine, and I kissed her fervently, my tongue dancing with hers, my hands pressing into her hips.

The taste of her mouth was even better knowing I'd get to taste it again and again for the next eight days.

Olivia pulled back, panting for breath. "So much for no feelings," she chuckled.

I laughed and sucked in a breath of my own. "I want as much time with you here as I can get," I whispered, leaning in to kiss her again.

She gasped and pulled back, but I could tell it was from excitement. "I almost forgot!"

She opened the mesh bag and pulled out a light blue shell that shimmered slightly in the low light. It was near perfect and fit right in her palm.

"I was collecting shells to take home, and I found this one." Holding it out to me with a smile, she added, "Your favorite color is blue, so it made me think of you.""

I blushed and took it from her, turning it around in my hand. "It's beautiful."

"Like you," Olivia said.

I looked up from the shell to her glowing face and smiled before slipping the shell into the pocket of my dress.

"Come here," I whispered, grabbing her hand and tugging her closer again.

Olivia slid her arm around my neck and leaned in to kiss me, her lips tasting of salt and fruit. My hand drifted to the small of her back, and I pressed myself closer to her.

As our kiss grew deeper, she moaned into my mouth, and I shivered and tugged at her bottom lip with my teeth. The scent of her skin, the taste of her lips, and the feeling of her warmth pressed to me were intoxicating.

"Let's get out of here," Olivia said into the kiss.

I hummed in agreement and reluctantly released her.

She took my hand, and we started away from the hut. After grabbing my things from where I'd been lounging with

Christa, Robert, and Liam—and ignoring Christa's smirking—I walked with Olivia back to her hotel room.

Once again in the elevator, we could barely keep our hands off each other, but this time, there was someone else with us. So, we were forced to hold hands until we made it to Olivia's floor.

"Let me get the door open!" Olivia giggled.

I had her pinned with her back against the wall beside her door and was trailing kisses along her neck. I could hear the card in her hand click as she brushed it against the door, trying to find the slot to unlock it.

"Never," I said playfully before capturing her mouth.

She kissed me back, warm and needy, but her hand was still desperately trying to get the door open.

Finally, the door beeped, and she pushed it open.

Olivia pulled me into the room, and I closed the door with my foot.

Her hands were all over me as she helped me get undressed, and my own fingers worked to peel off her cover up and bikini.

I was already panting for breath as she stepped back from me, naked, and stood at the end of the bed.

My eyes took in every inch of her tanned, curvy body. Strands of her hair fell in luxurious waves over her breasts.

Olivia's eyes were on me, too, hungry and passionate.

I watched as she slid onto the bed, further and further, until she was laying propped up by her elbows in the middle.

I crawled after her and hovered above her as she lowered her head to the bed. Her legs spread, and I rested between them, feeling heat radiate from her thighs.

"Kiss me," Olivia whispered.

Without hesitation, my lips moved against hers, slow and firm. I felt her breasts against mine, setting my whole body alight.

"I need you," I moaned into her mouth.

Olivia responded with a whine, and I felt her hips shift underneath me.

I understood immediately what she wanted and carefully changed my position. I pushed my hips down and felt Olivia's warm, wet pussy against mine.

As I rocked my hips, creating the friction we both desperately craved, I heard her gasp.

My clit throbbed as I rubbed my cunt against hers. The sound of her moans and the bed creaking quietly turned me on even more.

"Yes, yes," Olivia gasped. "Don't stop!"

I leaned up, grabbed the top of the headboard, and pushed my hips against her harder, faster.

"Fuck, fuck!" I cried.

Olivia rocked up against me, and our juices mixed, creating a delicious wet sound as we fucked.

I felt the pressure building so quickly inside me, I couldn't even vocalize it. My hips bucked harder, and I gripped at the headboard tighter as I came, a wave of pleasure crashing over me.

Even as the tingling of pleasure faded, I didn't stop. I wanted more. I wanted to make Olivia come, and I wanted to make her come hard.

Both of our bodies wiggled and squirmed against each other as we panted and moaned.

"That's it, Angel," I encouraged her. "Come for me."

Olivia arched her back, and I felt her shiver underneath me.

"I'm coming"!"

"Good Girl," I moaned. "Oh, God."

I tilted my head down and humped Olivia faster as I came again. My body went rigid, and a shiver ran up my spine as I gasped for air.

"Don't stop, please!" Olivia begged me.

My own clit was too sensitive to handle another orgasm, but I couldn't keep Olivia from another.

I moved again, resting between her thighs with my breasts pressed to hers.

She whined needily, but before those parted lips could get anything else out, I slid my hand down.

My fingers collected her wet arousal and caressed her clit.

Olivia's arms wrapped around me, and her nails bit into my back.

I groaned and rested my forehead against hers.

"Fuck," I sighed.

"Almost...th-there," Olivia moaned.

I rubbed her in quick, steady circles, feeling her body squirm underneath me.

With my free hand, I tilted her face to mine and kissed her deeply.

Her moans filled my mouth as we kissed, her tongue dancing around mine.

My heart drummed in my chest as I listened to her grow closer, and closer...until finally...

Olivia arched against me, her thighs squeezed me, and her mouth hung open, breathless for a second or two.

She slumped back down, panting for air and shaking.

"Oh...Kathleen." Olivia exhaled.

"Olivia," I whispered against her mouth.

DAE STORM

I nuzzled my face into the crook of her neck.
We laid like this for...who knows how long.
Everything felt perfect and timeless as I laid there with her.

7

Olivia

I was still lost in bliss even as the room cooled down and my heart slowed.

Kathleen sighed from her place on my neck, nuzzling and kissing every now and again.

I giggled softly.

She looked up at me with one eye, and nuzzled my jawline, then my cheek, before she kissed my lips once.

"You're like a kitten," I cooed, my heart squeezing in my chest.

Kathleen kissed my cheek. "Oh?"

"Yes," I smiled. "*Kitten.*"

The flush on her cheeks deepened. "I like that."

"Me, too." I giggled again.

I felt so utterly safe and sound cuddling with Kathleen. My legs tangled with hers as we laid there in the darkness.

Just as my bladder was screaming for attention, Kathleen rolled off me and onto her side.

"I need to go talk to the front desk," she told me.

I frowned. "Can't you do that tomorrow?" I rolled onto my side and gazed at her, not wanting to be away from her yet. I was still basking in the excitement of staying another week and getting more time with such an amazing woman.

"It's best if I do it tonight instead of before check-out tomorrow," Kathleen explained.

I pursed my lips and nodded. "That's true." Sighing, I sat up in bed. I needed some water, but first, the bathroom.

"Will you be back?" I asked.

Kathleen smiled at me, leaned over, and pressed her lips to mine, once, then twice.

"If you so desire."

My entire body was hot again at the low, husky tone of her voice.

"Of course," I replied.

"Then I will be back," she assured me.

My lips parted to speak, but she beat me to it.

"With food," she chuckled.

"Thanks," I said, and climbed off the bed.

I wasn't used to anything like my hookup with Kathleen, but if I wasn't careful, I could get very used to it.

※

I was lying on the bed, freshly washed, with damp hair, when there was a knock on the door. It'd been almost an hour since Kathleen left.

"It's me." Her voice was muffled through the door.

I groaned as I got up, secured the robe around my body out of habit, and opened the door.

"Hey! How'd it g—" I started, then saw Kathleen's furrowed brow.

"The clerk, as nice as she is, couldn't work anything out. There are no available rooms for the next week," she explained as she stepped into the room.

I closed the door behind her. My heart dropped into my stomach. "Oh, well... Maybe we can figure something else out." I wracked my brain, but I was too anxious about the idea of saying goodbye to her tomorrow to really think straight.

Kathleen's jaw was tight as she paced at the end of the bed.

"My boss has a whole fucking beach house," she mumbled, looking up at me.

"I remember," I sighed, my own brow furrowing. "I still can't believe he sent y'all here instead."

She nodded, and her eyes were darker as she looked away from me. "You know what..." She huffed and pulled her phone out.

"Huh?" I stepped closer.

Pressing the phone to her ear, she sat down on the end of the bed. I watched as she grumbled in frustration after a moment, hung up, and appeared to call again. Her knee bounced quickly.

"Hi, Kenneth," she said, her voice not at all pleased. "I don't care if you're in the middle of screwing someone, frankly. What I want to know is how in the hell could you think it's acceptable to send the four of us to a one bedroom, two-bed hotel room when you have a beach house just miles away?"

I could just barely hear the muffled and irritated voice of the man who must be Kenneth coming through the phone.

"No, you listen to me. I have been working for you for over a decade; so has Robert. You've treated us like scum for the last few years, and honestly, I'm tired of it." Kathleen stood up and paced in front of the bed again.

I watched with my arms folded, eyes wide, and pulse racing.

The way Kathleen continued to talk to her boss—angrily, but choosing her cutting words carefully—made my entire body hot and fuzzy. It was amazing seeing her stand up to him, even over the phone. I couldn't imagine talking to my boss that way, though from what I'd heard, my boss wasn't that bad compared to hers.

I stopped listening to her exact words, taking in her face, the way her brow furrowed, how her chest lifted with each breath, the darkness in her eyes, the sternness of her voice. I swallowed hard and shifted on my feet.

Finally, as her voice rose just a tad, I tuned back in.

"Sexism, homophobia, ableism, classism, sexual harassment...would you like me to go on?" she asked. Then she paused. "I didn't think so."

I bit my lip, wondering what Kenneth was saying, what was going to happen. Surely it couldn't end well.

"You're damn right you will," she replied, and her shoulders rolled back. "Good luck with that. Have a wonderful rest of your vacation." Her last words were laced with disgust.

The next second, she was tossing her phone onto the bed and taking a deep breath.

"What happened?" I asked. I stepped closer, my eyes so wide it almost hurt.

Kathleen took another breath before she answered. "We're staying in the beach house," she replied.

"Seriously?" I asked, bouncing a little in excitement.

She nodded. "I'm apparently fired as soon as this vacation is over, but for now, we get the fucking beach house." She grinned, but there was a pained look in her eyes.

My heart squeezed. "Oh God, you didn't need to do that!" I insisted. My head was all but spinning.

"I'm tired of working for that entitled narcissist anyway," she insisted, jaw tight. "No amount of money is worth it."

I raked my fingers through my damp hair and tried to grasp the situation. I decided to focus on the least anxiety-inducing aspect.

"God, Kathleen," I said with a chuckle. "That was...actually kind of hot."

My face flushed.

She smiled and stepped closer to me. "Anything to get another week with you," she told me. "Well, that, and not having to deal with him again. I can't control Robert or the others, but I'm done with that place."

"What are you going to do when you get back?" I asked, brow furrowed.

Kathleen shook her head. "I don't want to think about that now." She cupped my cheek. "All I want is you."

꙳

I couldn't contain my excitement or my anxiety as Kathleen and I lugged our things along the beach to Ken's beach house. Where were now and where the hotel was located were starkly different. The beach here was cleaner, the flora better taken care of, and the people that passed us were better dressed and held a certain aura about them that screamed "money."

"Don't tell me Ken keeps a key under the mat?" I joked.

Kathleen chuckled as we walked up the stairs to the front door. "No, but he keeps one in the key secured mailbox," she replied, punching a six-digit key into the small number pad on the front of the metal mailbox secured to the wall beside the door. She opened it and plucked out a glistening silver key..

"I can't believe he actually gave you the code," I marveled. "Are you sure your coworkers don't want to stay here too?" My stomach ached with guilt as Kathleen opened the door and the glossy wood floor in the foyer came into view.

Kathleen put the security code in after closing the door, and we both left our luggage in the foyer.

"Liam and Christa want nothing to do with me after telling Kenneth off, and Robert wants to give us privacy," she explained. She looked at me from over her shoulder, and I blushed.

"That makes sense," I said. I felt bad about Liam and Christa, but I also didn't know them. I wondered if I'd even meet them before the end of the week—or if I'd even want to.

I followed Kathleen further into the house. The living room was bigger than my entire hotel room. The windows were large and draped with light blue, floor-length curtains that the morning light filtered through lazily. Every single piece of floral art, cushy furniture, and shiny trinket looked like it was picked specifically for the house. However, the room lacked the warmth that a lived-in home might have.

"Wow, it's beautiful in here," I said.

When my eyes slid back to Kathleen, she was gazing at me with a heated look in her eyes.

"Not as beautiful as you." She smiled and stepped closer to me.

I bit my lip and stepped back from her playfully. "Oh, yeah?" I asked.

She chuckled and stepped closer still. "Mhm, and...we're all alone here. No one to hear you squirm and moan." She reached out to brush her fingers along my cheek.

My thighs squeezed together, and I stepped back again, this time tripping and falling back first onto the couch.

I laughed and reached a hand out, grabbing Kathleen's and pulling her down to me.

She laughed with me and settled between my thighs, her arms on either side of my head.

"Can't get enough of me, huh?" I giggled.

She leaned her head down and kissed the side of my neck. The warmth of her mouth tingled along my skin, and I hummed in pleasure.

"Why else would I beg you to stay another week?" she asked. Her nose nuzzled into the crook of my neck and I arched my back.

"Mm, I dunno, *Kitten*," I whispered.

Kathleen pushed her hips against me.

My fingers slid up and tangled into the back of her curls.

She sighed, then slowly kissed up my neck and jawline to my lips. I kissed her back, wrapping myself around her as much as I could.

Just as her hand slid up the front of my tank top with fingers wiggling along my soft stomach, said stomach growled aggressively.

Kathleen nipped my lip and asked, "Hungry, *Angel*?"

I blushed and licked my lips. "Mm, maybe a little," I replied.

She chuckled and moved off of me.

"No!" I insisted and tugged her back down.

"Let's get some food in you. Besides, didn't you want to try out the bathtub?" she asked.

I blinked. "Oh, right! Rich people have the best tubs." I laughed.

She moved off of me and stood up. I watched her for a second as she stretched her arms above her head. I sat up from the couch and did the same.

"Let's go get some lunch," Kathleen said, reaching out for my hand.

I nearly wiggled in excitement to still be in St. Lucia with a sexy, smart, and delicious woman.

❦

That first night in the beach house was incredible. The bath was massive and beyond relaxing, the porch had a perfect place to sit while Kathleen read aloud to me, and the bed was so comfortable that I fell asleep in minutes. I woke up earlier than I ever had on my own.

After a beach-side breakfast, Kathleen insisted we both put our bathing suits on and go waterfall hunting.

"I've never done this before," I admitted as I walked along the path beside Kathleen.

Trees towered over us, and the scent of damp wood and grass was strong and nostalgic somehow. We were several miles from the beach, in an area where it rained more frequently, making the forest lush.

As my fingers intertwined with Kathleen's, I found myself engrossed in the world surrounding us. Just as we reached a bend, and the sound of rushing water grew louder and louder, I heard chatter and the sound of laughter.

"Did we find it?" I asked.

"Yes, but we're not going to this one; it's too popular." Kathleen chuckled.

I looked over as we were passing the waterfall, and she was right. I could barely even see the water and the rocks with all the people standing there taking pictures.

"Alright, well, you lead the way." I smiled at her.

She smiled back at me and tugged me along.

I was careful not to trip over my own feet or face plant into any low-hanging branches, but Kathleen helped by pushing them to the side first and waiting for me to pass.

"You've been on a lot of island vacations?" I asked.

Kathleen hummed before answering. "Yes, and no. I grew up incredibly privileged. My family took a lot of vacations, but they weren't usually to places like this. I broke off on my own during college, was cut off from the money, and had to make my own way," she explained. "The company I work—worked for is a small, exclusive law firm, and they send their employees on vacation every year. It wasn't until the last few years that I started getting sent to island's with the rest of the outcasts, so to speak. This is the first year they actually didn't even bother to get more than one room."

I frowned. "Wow, well, I don't know if I'd even complain about an island," I admitted. "I had to pay for this all myself."

Kathleen nodded. "Not complaining about the island. It's beautiful. It's just...knowing the intentions that pisses me off."

"Must've been hard going from a family with money to all on your own with none," I said.

"It was, but I was already in college, and it only took a few years to find a really steady job because of my last name...even if my family, including all three of my siblings, had disowned me." She shrugged, but it was a sad gesture. "I was still much better off than others."

I was surprised at how self-aware Kathleen was. It only endeared me to her more.

"And you?" she asked. "I know you had to pay for the vacation on your own. You're a waitress, and you have no siblings."

I nodded. "My family is working class. My mother's still an elementary school teacher, and my dad still works at a construction company even though they're both at retirement age. When I was growing up, things were really rough, but they're doing good for themselves now."

"Would they help you if you asked?" Kathleen asked. "Just curious."

I stopped walking at looked over at her, brows furrowed. "Of course, but I don't ask. They need their money for them," I said. My voice was harsher than intended.

"Okay. I'm sorry if I hit a nerve," Kathleen replied, tugging me along gently to keep walking.

I took a slow breath, then smiled. "It's okay. I know there's nothing wrong with asking them for help, but I guess...I don't know." I shrugged.

She squeezed my hand tighter and was quiet for a moment as she led me through the trees until I could hear the rushing of water again, even louder this time.

As we emerged from the branches, glistening gray and blue rocks surrounding a small circle of shallow water came into view. The water splashed and bubbled as the waterfall met its surface and flowed under. Flowers stuck up from between moss-coverd rocks and lush grass. The sun poured down into the small space like it shone only there.

"Wow," I said. I couldn't get anything else out.

"Isn't it magnificent?" Kathleen asked, awestruck.

I was pretty sure I breathed out a "yeah," but it may have been only in my head.

"Come on," she said, pulling me forward.

"What?!" I laughed.

I rushed to keep up with Kathleen's pace as she led me to the waterfall. As she stepped in, the water immediately soaking her from head to toe, I held my breath and stepped in as well, not wanting to let go of her hand. Coming out from the other side, I giggled, the sound echoing around us in a surreal manner. Water dripped from my lashes as I looked at Kathleen, her curly hair clinging to the sides of her face and neck.

"Fuck, you're beautiful," I whispered.

I was grinning ear to ear as I stepped closer and tossed my arms around her neck. We were both dripping wet as I pulled myself tighter against her plush body. Droplets of water from the waterfall to the side of us splashed onto my calves every now and again.

"You are," she whispered back.

I couldn't help myself. I kissed her passionately and took in every single thing I could taste, smell, feel: the musky scent of her wet hair and skin, the fruity taste of her lips, the way she wrapped her arms tightly around me and kissed me deeper.

I moaned into her mouth and searched for something, anything, to lean on. The back of the small cave behind the waterfall was covered in green moss and vines, but I didn't care. I leaned back, pulling Kathleen with me as my back pressed against the cool, hard rock. Everything about her was sexy. The soft sounds that escaped her, her supple skin, and her rolls that squished against me.

"God, you drive me wild," I whispered against her mouth.

Kathleen chuckled breathlessly. "Show me."

I fervently pressed my lips against hers. No care in the world was great enough to pull me from that moment. My skin was so hot, I couldn't stand it, and the water droplets on my arms, neck, and face all but evaporated into the surrounding air.

"You sure you want me to show you?" I asked, looking up at her longingly.

A needy, passionate look heated Kathleen's eyes. "Yes, Angel.""

Blushing even deeper, I ducked under her arm and dashed away. She looked at me, confused, but I wordlessly rushed over to the waterfall, turning back to her as I stepped beneath it. I gasped, laughing as the cold water flooded down my back. Squeezing my eyes shut, I tilted my head back and shook my hair as the water poured over my face.

"You make me so hot!" I delightedly shouted over the roar of the waterfall. "I need this!"

I could barely see Kathleen through the water in front of my eyes as it dripped down over my forehead, but I could just barely hear her laughter echoing around me. But I reached a hand out, and she took it. As I pulled her into the waterfall, she let go so her hands could capture my face, and she kissed me deeper than ever before as we were drenched by the cold, refreshing shower.

8

Kathleen

The week went by far too quick. Waterfall hunting, sight-seeing, and countless bubble baths were just part of the fun Olivia and I had together. By the time the day before we would have to part came along, I was utterly engrossed in her, mind, body, and soul.

But not everything was going as well.

"I'm sorry about Christa and Liam," Robert said.

I walked beside him as he wheeled up the small ramp to the side of the stairs of the beach house.

"I don't expect everyone to be okay with my choices," I replied. "Besides, they'll figure out it isn't worth kissing Kenneth's ass. Eventually."

Robert chuckled, and I opened the door for him.

Introducing Robert to Olivia had been something I was uncertain about the entire time we had been hooking up. I had only had casual hookups and relationships a handful of times in my life, and never had I ever introduced any of them—not including my ex-wife—to my coworkers. Maybe it was the fact that it might never happen after today that prompted me to give into Olivia's interest of finding out even more about my life. Or maybe...maybe it was something else. I didn't want to think about that too much.

"We're here!" I called from the foyer as I closed the door behind Robert. "Hello?" I asked after I heard nothing, raising one eyebrow.

"Ah!" Olivia laughed as she rushed into the foyer. "I was just taking the snacks outside."

"Oh, yes." I said, chuckling.

It was silent for a long moment before I finally looked down at Robert and waved a hand at him. "Olivia, this is Robert; Robert, this is Olivia."

He reached out towards Olivia. She looked at him uncertainly for a second, like she hadn't shaken someone's hand before, then shuffled forward and shook his hand with a smile.

"It's nice to meet you, Robert," she said. "I hear you've worked with Kathleen for a while?"

I followed behind the two of them as they made their way out of the foyer toward the deck with its seamless pool.

"Ten years now. Kathy worked there before me," Robert replied, excitement in his voice. He loved meeting anyone from my life, which wasn't often. I kept work and home very separate.

"That's great! I can't even imagine what being a lawyer is like I've been a waitress since high school," Olivia replied.

"Yeah, it's a shame Kathy won't be there anymore. A waitress, really?"

My pulse thudded in my temples as I listened to them. We all made it out onto the deck, and I sat down in a lounge chair as the two of them continued to chat.

"No offense meant, but you're a lot younger than I expected," Robert said.

I nearly choked. Olivia's face flushed deeply, and her eyes met mine for a moment.

"I'm twenty-seven," she told him. "Twenty-eight in December. She didn't tell you?"

Robert laughed. "No! I was shocked when she asked for me to come over and hang out."

Olivia laughed as well. Meanwhile, I was pink, and my arms were folded over my chest.

"Alright, it's not that big of a difference," I insisted. "Seventeen years. Isn't your mother twenty years older than your father, Rob?" My voice was slightly defensive.

Robert smiled sheepishly. "Point taken."

Olivia shifted on her feet, and I saw her teeth sink into her lip the way it did when she was nervous or very excited. "Let's get in the pool, yeah?" she suggested.

I stood up from the chair and slid my sandals off, pulling my cover-up over my head. After helping Robert into the pool, Olivia and I slid in after him. Tingles ran up my spine as she intertwined her fingers with mine under the water.

"Ah, this is nice," Olivia sighed.

"It's better than the hotel pool, that's for sure," Robert agreed.

I nodded. I wasn't going to mention the whole situation with the hotel, being fired...not seeing Olivia again after tomorrow. It was just easier. Or at least, I was trying to convince myself it was. But the universe had other plans.

"I can't believe y'all were treated like that," Olivia said.

Robert shook his head. "You know, it's been going on so long, I guess I just got used to it," He paused for a moment. "But you know what? I'm done, too."

I blinked. "What?"

"When we get back to New York, I'm quitting," Robert explained. "Christa and Liam may not want to get in the middle of it, but if you're done dealing with it, so am I. We can both put up a fight."

"You don't have to do that," I insisted, leaning forward slightly so I could better see his face.

"I do. We're the best damn lawyers they got, and they treat us like trash! It's time we both find a better place."

My eyes burned slightly with tears. "I'll help you with finding another job. It's the least I can do."

"Thanks," he said, sniffling a little.

I looked over at Olivia, who looked even more teary eyed than me. "Oh, hell." She chuckled. "I'm going to grab those snacks off the table for us."

I smiled at her and squeezed her hand, then reluctantly let it go so she could get out of the pool. My eyes met Robert's for a moment, and for the first time in a long time, I knew who was really my friend.

❧

"Think you can find something better than the one I found you?" Olivia asked with a playful smile.

I rolled my eyes. "Never," I insisted, "But I'm sure we could find some nice ones."

After a few hours of hanging out with Robert and getting as water-wrinkled as possible, Olivia led me out to the beachfront for a stroll and a seashell hunt. Our clasped hands swung gently between our bodies as we walked along the sand, our sandals kicking up dust behind us. The waves crashed beside us, the sound and smell relaxing. I looked over at the setting sun and realized we were right back where we were two weeks before when we first met. Walking along the beach at sunset...

I swallowed my disappointment at it being the last time.

As Olivia let go of my hand and went shuffling over to brush around in the sand, my fingers wiggled uncomfortably in her absence. I smiled, though, watching her rummage around.

"First one to find an unbroken purple shell, wins!" Olivia shouted gleefully.

"Hey, that's not fair! You got a head start!"

My glance darted around, my fingers brushing sand and water off various shells. I found a purple shell, but it was only half of one. I cursed under my breath. I would have never been interested in this with anyone else. Hell, I wouldn't have even thought of it. But in that moment, I was excited to find the complete purple shell before Olivia, to playfully rub it in her face and see her smile.

Just as I was considering giving up, I spotted purple out of the corner of my eye—a very light purple, but purple it was.

I dashed towards it, fixing the strap of my dress. Then I realized Olivia was headed in the same direction.

I picked up the pace, but so did she, both of our hands aimlessly trying to get the damn thing out of the sand before the other could.

Olivia giggled. "It's mine!"

I couldn't help the laughter from bubbling out of my throat. She just made me so damn happy. A paler hand than mine plucked it up, and I saw it was indeed an unbroken, pastel purple shell.

"Yes!" Olivia threw the hand with the shell into the air.

I grinned at her. "Alright, you win," I said.

"Aw, yeah," she crowed and did a little dance, moving her hips in a circle and her fists in a similar rotation.

I covered my hand with my mouth and laughed, my face red, my brain overflowing with serotonin. As I watched her dance, her blonde hair blowing in the ocean breeze, my stomach suddenly tightened. My eyes burned with tears. My throat was so tight it hurt.

"Olivia," I choked out.

She stopped dancing and looked at me, her eyes laced with concern, brows furrowed in confusion. "You alright?" she asked, suddenly at my side.

"I don't want to never see you again," I told her, my voice thick with emotion.

Olivia's face slowly contorted in her own pain slowly as she grasped what I'd said. "Kathleen..." she whispered.

I swallowed hard. "I want you to be more than a summer fling," I admitted. "I've never felt happier than these last two weeks."

Olivia's own eyes glittered with tears that threatened to fall onto her cheeks. I wanted to hold her, wanted to even just reach a hand out, but I waited.

"Me too," she said, "you make me so happy. I thought maybe it was just the beach, the sun, but...I feel like I could be just as happy with you in the middle of Alaska."

I laughed, eyes blurring, "And you'd hate it there."

She laughed as well, then sniffled. "But our lives are so different. You're in New York, and I'm in the middle-of-nowhere Ohio. I would never make it in New York."

I nodded in understanding, my eyes falling to the sand. Then my pulse doubled as I said, "I'll find a new job in Ohio.""

Olivia's eyes widened. "What?"

"When I get back to New York, I'm out of a job. I have so few friends there. And no family. I'll move to Ohio, find a job there, and start over."

Olivia's tears finally spilled over. "A-are you sure?" she asked. "We've only known each other two weeks. Would you really do that?"

"Yes. I'm serious about this. I don't care what anyone else thinks. I've spent so much of my life taking the safest route. And I'm done." I squeezed her hands. "I want to be in your life." My voice cracked. "If you'll have me."

Olivia hiccupped softly. "Yes, of course! I want to be in your life, too."

I let go of her hands and wrapped my arms around her, kissing her deeply. Tears dripped down my face and mixed with hers, salty, sweet.

The emotions I felt were overwhelming, but it felt so right to give Olivia every bit of affection I had. I broke the kiss, slowly kissing down her neck, nibbling and flicking my tongue along her skin.

"Angel." I sighed into the crook of her neck.

Olivia trailed kisses along my jawline, and a shiver ran up my back. I sunk my teeth gently into her shoulder, and she whined.

"Take me home," she whispered.

I didn't hesitate. Grabbing her hand, I dragged her as quickly and gently as possible towards the beach house.

My first goal was the bedroom, but as soon as the door was closed and the code put in, Olivia was on me. Her hands trailed up my hips, tugging my dress over my head until I was in just my bikini. I grabbed her face and kissed her, pressing her back against the wall beside the door. Her teeth nipped at my bottom lip.

"I need you," I said between breaths.

I slid my hands down, pulling her own cover-up off and tossing it to the floor. We left a trail of clothing down the hallway into the living room as we went, our kisses heated and urgent the whole way. Olivia collapsed onto the couch and brought me down with her, our naked bodies pressed to each other. I felt every inch of her against me, and it only made me more wet.

"*Kitten*," she whispered.

I moaned as our mouths met again, my hips resting between her legs. So often we seemed to wind up like this—me on top—and it felt comfortable, natural, for us.

As Olivia ardently kissed me, our tongues swirling together, I slid a hand down her body to her hot, wet pussy, which never failed to be ready for me. I collected her juices with my fingers and slowly slid two of them inside of her. She moaned into my mouth, her hips rocking against my hand and forearm. I pumped my fingers in and out, over and over, ignoring my own cunt's aching need as I pleasured her.

"Oh, yes!" she cried. "Don't stop!"

"That's it. *Good girl*," I whispered. "Rock your hips for me."

My words spurred her on, and I felt her shiver beneath me and push up harder. My thumb found her clit, circling it quickly as my fingers thrust in and out of her needy pussy.

"Yes...fuck, yes, so close!" Olivia arched against my body, rolling her hips desperately.

I bit at her shoulder, applying pressure as I fingered her, and felt her tense again, and again.

Her moans became breathless, no words able to escape as I drove her to the edge of her orgasm and let her fall over. I felt her squeeze against my fingers, and I pushed them as deep inside as I could, curling my fingers a bit more. Olivia gasped for air as her arched and tensed body finally relaxed into the couch.

I pulled my fingers out of her and stuck them in my mouth, sucking her delicious, musky juices from them before kissing up her jawline. Olivia's face turned, her lips searching for mine. My tongue slid into her mouth, and she moaned and rubbed up against me as she got a taste of herself.

I felt her legs shift underneath me, and I followed her lead, moving until our pussies were flush against each other with just a tilt of our hips. My slick, wet arousal mingled with hers, and I shivered as her nails brushed down my back.

I wanted to give her just a few more seconds to rest, but Olivia rocked her hips before I could.

At the tingling friction against my clit, I moaned and rolled my hips and thighs in time with her. Our movements were slow and passionate, our foreheads pressed together, our breaths syncing.

"Oh...Kathleen," Olivia moaned and shivered.

"Olivia." I pushed against her more firmly.

As our bodies caressed each other's, I slowly inched toward orgasm. I wanted it so badly, but I also wanted this to last as long as it could.

Olivia and I in the room's dimness, the soft couch under her back and her warm, soft, beautiful body underneath me...

"Come for me," Olivia whispered, her fruity breath tickling my lips and cheeks.

I moaned, and my brow furrowed as I focused on doing as she told me. "Cum with me, Angel," I begged. "Please."

We gasped at the same time, our hips rolling into each other in perfect synchronicity.

My pussy throbbed and my clit ached as I drew closer and closer to going over the edge.

A shiver rushed up my back, and waves of pleasure rolled down my thighs to my toes. I felt Olivia's body stiffen under mine, her cunt pulsing against my own as we both came.

"Oh...fuck!" Olivia gasped.

"Fuck...fuck..." I moaned, my head sliding into her neck, my voice muffled by her ear.

My hips shivered and bucked against her, and I felt her thighs squeeze me like a vise. Finally, we both exhaled and relaxed against each other. I leaned my head back up and kissed her lips softly, once, then twice. Olivia's eyes were half open as she caught her breath. I looked into her eyes as I steadied myself, beads of sweat dripping from my hairline and into her own damp hair.

The room was muggy and smelled unmistakably of sex.

Olivia laughed softly.

"What?" I asked, smiling.

"I get to see you again," she whispered. "And do this again."

I chuckled and rubbed my nose against hers. "Oh, god,, yes. Over and over."

Olivia sighed and closed her eyes.

I kissed her nose and cheeks, watching as her closed-mouth smile grew bigger.

After a moment, however, she frowned.

"We need to pack for the flight in the morning," she reminded me.

I blinked. "Ah, yes."

I smiled. "Don't forget your purple shell, winner."

Olivia laughed and gently shoved me. Everything about that moment was perfect.

I couldn't wait to see where we would be a year from now.

Epilogue - Olivia

"**A**h, damnit!"

I huffed as the second pair of pantyhose I'd put on ripped at the thigh. I snatched them off my body and tossed them in a ball to the side. Fuck it, I didn't need any. I had wanted to dress fancier for Kathleen's and my anniversary, but I knew she'd probably prefer it if I wore nothing under my dress anyhow. I smirked at the thought, but then my pulse quickened.

One-year anniversary. Is it really that time already?

Kathleen had moved to Ohio a week after quitting her job in New York and helping Robert find another job. I'd moved in with her just three months ago. Time felt like it had flown by but, at the same time, like it was moving slower than ever.

I clutched one of my heels to my chest as I sat on the end of our bed.

"Are we moving too fast?" I asked out loud. I'd never felt so happy with anyone, but could it be like that forever?

The dark wooden figure, curving and glistening, caught my attention from where it sat on the dresser. One either side of it were two shells, one blue and one purple. I smiled as my heart thudded quicker.

Kathleen had gotten be the statue for our six month anniversary, and it made be just as happy now as it did then.

I felt a soft familiar brush against my ankle, and I looked down, pulled out of my thoughts.

"Hi, sweet baby," I cooed, reaching down to stroke the side of Grape's face and ears.

Grape purred at me and continued to nuzzle my legs.

"Mommy Two will be home from work soon," I insisted. "Then we're going to dinner."

Grape meowed and bonked his head against my calf.

"I know, I know. We won't be gone too long."

After a whole five minutes of disassociating while petting my cat, I finally finished getting dressed. My hair was done up in a twist at the back of my head, several waves of hair framing my face. My heels clicked against the hardwood floor as made my way out of the bedroom. Just as I rounded the corner into the kitchen, I heard the front door open. My pulse quickened, and I shuffled down the hallway toward the sound of jingling keys.

"You're home!" I beamed.

As Kathleen closed the door and turned to face me, I crashed into her and wrapped my arms around her neck.

"Yeah, I had to—" she started, but I cut her off.

My mouth claimed hers with no hesitation. I felt her tense shoulders relax under my arms and her own hands slide onto my hips. She kissed me back, slow and deep. I was lost in her for God knows how long before I finally pulled back to look into her gray eyes.

"Mm, hello *Angel*," Kathleen whispered.

I shivered and stood up taller to rub my nose against hers. "Hi," I giggled. I took in her face and saw the darkening circles under her eyes and the way her curls were out of place. "Oh, you look tired." I frowned. "Are you sure that you want to go out tonight?"

Kathleen pecked my lips. "We must. You look too sexy to stay inside."

My face flushed, but I held my ground. "We can go out any night," I insisted, patting her blazer. "We can push the reservation to tomorrow and stay in tonight. Order some takeout."

Kathleen sighed. "Baby, you really don't have to do that. You spent all this time getting ready after work."

I smiled at her and slid my hand down her arm to grab her hand. "I know. But I've missed you all day; I want to keep you all to myself."

We both slipped off our shoes near the front door, and I towed Kathleen, who was no longer resisting, toward the couch.

"You just sit, and I'll order the food." I leaned down to kiss her.

Before I could get away, Kathleen was pulling me closer and kissing me harder. I gasped softly into the kiss as she tugged me into her lap. I straddled her, my red dress sliding up my thighs. My fingers slid along the three open buttons of her shirt, and I nearly purred at feeling her warm chest against my hand.

Her lips left mine and slid down my jawline to my neck. Heat fluttered in my thighs as she trailed kisses from my neck to my shoulder. Her fingers tugged the neckline of my dress to the side.

"*Kitten*," I crooned.

"My *Angel*." Kathleen's breath brushed along my neck and I shivered.

I rocked my hips softly against her lap, wishing my dress and her skirt were already on the floor. She had such a way of making me care about nothing but being close to her. Just as I was about to suggest the bedroom—screw the food—Kathleen kissed up my neck and pulled back.

"Let me order the food; you make yourself comfortable." She kissed my lips one more time before gently coaxing me off her lap.

I hummed in defiance but slid off her lap onto the cushion beside her. I watched as she grabbed her phone and stepped into the kitchen to pull out one of our takeout menus.

"Thai?" she asked.

"That sounds good. You know what I like." I smiled and stood up from the couch, walking to the bedroom.

Just in case she was looking at me, I reached behind me and undid the claw clip from my hair, letting it fall down my back and shoulders. I peeked behind my shoulder to see her staring at me hungrily, then I snickered and disappeared into the bedroom.

Kathleen's voice was a quiet sound through the apartment. I looked around for Grape, but he wasn't in the room. He was most likely in his cat tree bed in Kathleen's home office on the other side of the living room. With a chuckle, I tossed the claw-clip onto the dresser and shook my hair out more. Just as I was reaching behind me to unzip my dress, I felt Kathleen's hand over mine.

"I got it," she whispered.

I pulled my hand away, and my skin tingled as her fingers slowly unzipped my dress all the way down to the small of my back. She brushed her fingers up to the nape of my neck, and I felt her breath against my shoulder as she eased the dress off my arms and down my hips.

"You're so beautiful, my love," she said huskily.

I shivered, stepping out of the dress and letting it fall to the floor before turning around to face her. She was so beautiful in her lilac blouse, dark blue blazer, and pencil skirt; her clothing hugged her wide curves perfectly.

"You're gorgeous." I sighed.

As I stood there in only my panties and strapless bra, I reached over and helped her slide her blazer off. My fingers gently unbuttoned her shirt and slid it off her arms to the floor. Her breasts were held snuggly by her bra, and I brushed my fingertips along the fabric.

I was distracted by her beauty, and the next moment she'd tossed her skirt and pantyhose to the floor.

I wrapped my arms around her neck again and pulled myself closer to her. "Are you sure you're not too tired?" I whispered.

Kathleen kissed me softly, then spoke against my lips. "Tired or not, I want you."

That was all I needed to hear. I kissed her passionately, slowly backing up to the bed until I crashed into it and fell onto my back. Kathleen helped us slide further onto the bed. I giggled as I rested my head on a pillow. She looked down at me, eyes tired but needy.

"Food will be here in thirty minutes," she told me right before her mouth was on my throat.

"Mm, not long enough," I teased.

She slid a hand under my back and popped the hooks of my bra open before sliding it off my body and flinging it onto the floor on the other side of the bed. I gasped as her tongue found one of my nipples and swirled around the hardening bud. My head fell back against the pillow as I arched against her. I wanted to tell her how much I had missed her all day, how much I loved her, but I couldn't get the words out of my mouth. My head was already too dizzy.

She sucked gently at my nipple, then licked her way over to my other breast.

I slid my hands up her back to unhook her own bra and slowly drew it off her body.

"Come here," I whispered.

With our breasts pressed against each other's, I leaned my head up to kiss her. Her lips were sweet and warm, and our mouths fit so perfectly together, like romantic marble statues created only to exist in each other's embrace.

As we kissed, my thighs spread, and she rested between them; the only thing between us were our panties. My thighs were hot.

"You make me so wet, baby," I crooned.

Kathleen moaned into our kiss and pressed tighter to me. At that moment, there was no one and nothing else in the world. All I wanted was her.

My arousal grew hotter and needier as Kathleen rubbed against me and brushed her tongue against mine.

"I need you," she whispered against my mouth.

I squirmed underneath her and threaded my fingers into the back of her hair.

"I need you, too, please," I begged, my legs squeezing around her.

Kathleen deepened our kiss for just a second before she slid away from me, and I stared as she pulled her panties off, tantalized by the lush curves of her stomach and thighs. Biting my lip when she leaned forward and hooked her fingers into the waistband of my panties, I shifted my hips and let her pull them off me.

I felt the cooler air of the room against me and shivered. Sighing and closing my eyes, I heard a quiet click, then I felt Kathleen's lubed fingers slide along my labia and slowly push inside me. I moaned as my hips pushed against her thrusting fingers, but she removed her fingers after only a few thrusts, and I whined softly.

"Patience, *Angel*," she whispered. She gave a low chuckle, and the sound made me shiver again as my clit throbbed.

I opened my eyes to see her sliding one end of our double ended vibrator into her pussy and then positioning herself between my legs again. My heart pounded, and I could barely keep myself still. I giggled softly and circled my arms around her neck again, pulling her down to me.

Kathleen laughed softly with me. "Hold on baby," she said. She reached down, and I felt the other end of the vibrator fill me, then vibrate at a low and steady pace.

"Mm." I grabbed Kathleen by the hair at the nape of her neck and kissed her desperately.

As my hips bucked, she rocked against me, thrusting the vibrator further inside both of us with each roll of our hips.

"Oh fuck." I pulled my legs up and wrapped them around Kathleen, bringing myself closer to her until our breasts were pressed together.

Every moan and pant that came from her mouth drove me wild.

She broke our kiss, and her lips slid down my jawline and neck. As her teeth bit into my shoulder, my hips pushed up against her. I was coming before I even realized it, my pussy squeezing the vibrator as my back arched.

" Kathleen!" I gripped her tighter.

She shivered against me, her hips thrusting harder. "Oh, fuck, Olivia," she moaned.

As my orgasm ended and I quickly built up to another, I used the leverage of my legs around her and rolled us over, bringing Kathleen onto her back.

She gasped as I slipped between her beautiful thighs and rolled my hips against her. My clit throbbed as my juices dripped between us.

"That's it, baby," I panted. "Come on, Kitten; come for me."

I grasped the headboard, my breasts in her face. Kathleen moaned beneath me, her mouth wrapping around one of my nipples and sending me shivering and aching for her. I rocked my hips harder against her, my pussy so close to hers.

"*Angel*," she moaned against my breast. "I'm...coming!"

Her words sent me right over the edge of my own orgasm, and my body went rigid, just as hers did. A string of words I wasn't even sure of escaped my mouth as my hips shivered and stuttered against hers. Finally, I relaxed and let go of the headboard. I sunk down against Kathleen's body and panted for breath.

My lips searched for hers until they met, and she kissed me back softly. I felt her hands stroke up and down my back and over the curve of my ass.

"I love you so much," I whispered.

Kathleen brushed her nails along my back, eliciting a small moan. "I love you too," she replied.

I giggled, my heart feeling full. "Happy Anniversary," I sighed, "I want to be with you forever."

There was a moment of silence, and I pressed my forehead against hers.

"Marry me," Kathleen said.

My heart stopped for a split second. "What?"

Kathleen shifted underneath me until she was sitting up and I was in her lap, the vibrator sliding out of both of us and onto the bed.

"What's happening?" I asked, my head dizzy as she struggled to reach over to the nightstand.

When she pulled her arm back over to me, I realized there was a blue velvet ring box in her hand. My hand immediately went to my mouth.

"Olivia, my love, my *Angel*, will you make me the happiest woman in the world and allow me to be your wife?"

Tears welled in my eyes. "Oh, Kathleen!" I sobbed softly. "Yes, I want to be your wife! Of course I'll marry you!"

Kathleen's eyes were laced with tears as well. "Thank God!"

She sighed, and I gave my hand to her, letting her slide the ring on my finger. It fit perfectly.

"Oh, you're sneaky," I teased her, sniffling. "I wish I could actually see it!" I wiped at my eyes, trying to clear the blur.

Kathleen laughed and pulled me tight against her, kissing all over my face, again and again. All my worries from earlier in the evening were gone I knew without a doubt that she was the woman I wanted to spend forever with.

Me, Kathleen, and Grape, forever.

Acknowledgments

To **Gabriel,** the absolutely wonderful editor who proofread this novella, and pumped me up the entire way to getting this published. I so appreciate you more than I can express!

I also would not have been able to get this done if it weren't for the late evening writing sprints in the Spicy Discord server, you know who you are; but special thanks to **A** and **C** for being so incredibly friendly, supportive, and ass-kicking with getting things done. I love you all!

To **M**, my rock, and my biggest fan. I could write nothing if it weren't for your constant support in so many ways.

Coming Summer 2023

Keep an eye out for next year's sapphic summer story

Rockstar Summer

If you would like to be on my ARC team and receive **Advanced Reader Copies** of all of my releases, sign up at the link below:

https://booksprout.co/reviewer/team/25716/dae-storm-readers

Made in the USA
Monee, IL
11 August 2022

11307252R00067